This was the reason Takis was having to marry. This uncontrollable desire that he'd never felt so intensely for any other woman.

He had been unable to resist Lissa's sensual allure, and their one perfect night had resulted in Lissa's conceiving his child, changing the course of his life.

But he *would* control his body's response to her that made his heart rate quicken and his blood thunder through his veins. He was determined that their marriage would be on his terms.

"We will live in Greece," he told her. "Do you have any preferences on the kind of house you would like?"

"So I am to have a choice?"

He narrowed his eyes at her sarcastic tone.

"I don't mind living in Greece. But I want us to discuss things. I am an adult, not a child who you can tell what to do," Lissa said with some asperity. "Marriage is about compromise."

"I will try to remember," he said evenly. *Compromise* was not a word in Takis's vocabulary, but he would put his ring on Lissa's finger and thereby claim his child before she discovered that fact.

Innocent Summer Brides

Now pronounced...a Greek's wife!

The Buchanan sisters, Eleanor and Lissa, own and run the family boutique hotel portfolio along with their brother. And the luxury Greek island resort the Panaglos hotel is the jewel in their property crown. Only now they face losing it!

In fighting to save it, the two sisters find themselves face-to-face with two gorgeous yet enigmatic Greeks. And discover that the passion burning bright between them can lead in only one direction—down the aisle...

Discover why in...

Eleanor's story
The Greek Wedding She Never Had

&

Lissa's story
Nine Months to Tame the Tycoon

Both available now!

Chantelle Shaw

NINE MONTHS TO TAME THE TYCOON

HARLEQUIN
PRESENTS

HARLEQUIN
PRESENTS

Recycling programs
for this product may
not exist in your area.

ISBN-13: 978-1-335-56796-3

Nine Months to Tame the Tycoon

Copyright © 2021 by Chantelle Shaw

This edition published by arrangement with Harlequin Books S.A.

For questions and comments about the quality of this book,
please contact us at CustomerService@Harlequin.com.

Harlequin Enterprises ULC
22 Adelaide St. West, 40th Floor
Toronto, Ontario M5H 4E3, Canada
www.Harlequin.com

Printed in U.S.A.

Chantelle Shaw lives on the Kent coast and thinks up her stories while walking on the beach. She has been married for over thirty years and has six children. Her love affair with reading and writing Harlequin stories began as a teenager, and her first book was published in 2006. She likes strong-willed, slightly unusual characters. Chantelle also loves gardening, walking and wine.

Books by Chantelle Shaw

Harlequin Presents

The Virgin's Sicilian Protector
Reunited by a Shock Pregnancy
Wed for the Spaniard's Redemption
Proof of Their Forbidden Night
Her Wedding Night Negotiation
Housekeeper in the Headlines

Innocent Summer Brides

The Greek Wedding She Never Had

Secret Heirs of Billionaires

Wed for His Secret Heir

Visit the Author Profile page
at Harlequin.com for more titles.

For Adrian

We met on your sixteenth birthday. Still going strong on your sixtieth.

That's a lot of love!

CHAPTER ONE

'I DID NOT expect to find you out here alone in the dark.'

Lissa Buchanan tensed when a gravelly voice with a sexy Greek accent came from the shadows. She knew without turning her head that the voice belonged to Takis Samaras and her skin prickled.

'I thought you would still be holding court in the marquee,' he drawled. 'The most beautiful woman on the dance floor attracting the attention of every man in the room.'

'I wasn't trying to attract attention.' She was aware that she sounded defensive. She hated the party girl label the tabloids had given her. Her reputation in the media was not the real Lissa Buchanan, but she was not about to explain that to a stranger, even though he was the most intriguing man she had ever met. Her pulse rate had accelerated at Takis's casual compliment. 'Besides, my sister is the most beautiful woman at her wedding.'

'Eleanor is a delightful bride, which I assume is

the reason Jace chose her for his wife,' Takis said drily.

'You seem surprised about Jace's marriage to my sister.' Lissa finally dared to look at Takis and nothing could have prepared her for her reaction to his potent masculinity. Never before had she felt such an intense sexual attraction. Beneath her bridesmaid's dress her nipples were hard, and the silk scraped across the sensitive peaks, creating a delicious friction.

The wedding ceremony had taken place at the town hall in Thessaloniki earlier in the day. Lissa's heart had missed a beat when she'd set eyes on Jace Zagorakis's best man. She had been conscious of his brooding presence and barely able to concentrate while Eleanor and Jace had made their vows.

Throughout the reception that was being held in a large marquee in the garden of Jace's beachfront house, Lissa had found her gaze constantly drawn to Takis. He was not conventionally handsome. Tall and powerfully muscular, but his chiselled face bore a grimly forbidding expression. On the rare occasions when he smiled, his teeth were a flash of brilliant white against his olive-toned skin. His jet-black hair was cropped short and beneath heavy brows his eyes were the colour of cold steel.

There was something uncompromising and at the same time fascinating about his mouth, which was both sensual and cruel. He was sleek and in the prime of physical fitness and he reminded Lissa of a wolf.

He shrugged. 'I confess I did not expect that Jace would marry. I have known him for a long time, and he has always been against marriage.'

'Ah, but who can understand the mystery of love?' she murmured.

'You think *love* is the reason why Jace's marriage to your sister took place at short notice?'

'What other reason could there be?' Lissa looked towards the main part of the garden, which was illuminated by hundreds of fairy lights, and saw Eleanor and her new husband emerge from the marquee. It was obvious that they only had eyes for each other. She sensed that Takis was about to say something, but he hesitated as his gaze followed hers over to the newlyweds.

'Perhaps you are right. I am not an expert on love,' he said in a cynical voice.

Lissa looked away from him, wondering why he disturbed her so strongly. She had sought a reprieve from socialising and taken refuge in a secluded corner of the garden where she could hear the soothing sound of the waves lapping against the shore on the other side of the wall.

She sensed that Takis had moved nearer to her, and he rested his elbow on the wall, trapping her against the old stones. She wasn't really trapped, but her feet seemed to be welded to the ground. His close proximity increased her awareness of the heat emanating from his body. Her eyes were drawn to him of their own volition, and she noticed the shadow of dark chest hairs beneath his white silk shirt. The spicy scent of his aftershave evoked a tug of response in the pit of her stomach.

'You have not told me why you left the party.'

She certainly wasn't going to admit that she'd felt envious when she'd watched him dance with a voluptuous brunette who looked as though she had been poured into her scarlet dress. 'I came outside because I want to be alone.'

'Liar,' he said softly. 'Do you think I hadn't noticed you staring at me at the reception?'

Had she been that obvious? Lissa's insides squirmed with embarrassment. He was the sexiest man she had ever encountered. The men she knew were mostly good-looking models or wannabe actors, but compared to Takis they were boys. He would be an incredible lover. She did not know how she could be so certain, given her complete lack of sexual experience, but the ache low in her pelvis was a response to his smouldering sensuality.

She prayed that the darkness hid the blush she felt spread across her face. 'Are you suggesting I came out here hoping you would follow me?'

'Did you?'

'Of course not. I didn't realise you had noticed me. You were being eaten alive by the woman in the too-tight dress.'

Takis laughed and the husky sound was unexpected and utterly captivating. 'I apologise for disturbing your solitude. I'll go away if you wish.' He spoke with the confidence of a man who was fully aware of his effect on the opposite sex, of his effect on *her*.

'You can do what you want. I'm sure you will anyway.' It would be a dangerous mistake to believe that a wolf could be tamed, Lissa decided. 'Feel free to stay here and watch the moonlight on the sea. I'm going up to the house to wait for my taxi.'

'I believe you are staying at the Pangalos Beach Resort tonight. I am also staying at the hotel and it makes sense for me to drive you.'

The journey to Sithonia, a peninsula in northern Greece, took over an hour from Thessaloniki. The prospect of being alone with Takis shredded Lissa's composure, but she could not think of an excuse to refuse to go with him. 'Um…that's kind of you.' She did not recognise the husky voice as her own.

He shrugged. 'Jace gave me the responsibility of ensuring that you reach your hotel safely.'

So he had only offered to drive her because it was his duty as best man and not because he was interested in her. Not that she wanted him to be, Lissa assured herself. But she hated the idea that she was a liability, which was exactly how her grandfather had made her feel when she'd been growing up.

'I am not kind,' Takis told her. 'Do not confuse me with your boyfriends with rich daddies who you have fooled around with on a beach in the Maldives or on a yacht in St Tropez. Your love life is an endless source of entertainment for anyone who reads the tabloids.' His jaw hardened. 'I am a survivor. I dragged myself out of a gutter and fought every step of the way to build my successful hotel chain.'

Lissa was infuriated by his sarcastic comments. How dared he judge her, especially as he did not know the first thing about her. She was about to tell him that it was no business of his how she lived her life. But she did not owe him an explanation.

She'd had years of practice at hiding her true feelings and gave a languid shrug as she forced herself to meet Takis's gaze. 'Presumably, *you* read the gutter press as you seem to know so much about me.'

In fairness she could not blame him for thinking the worst of her. She had never denied the rumours and gossip about her private life, and in fact she had deliberately sought the attention of the media, knowing that reports of her alleged bad behaviour were bound to infuriate her grandfather. One way or another she had been determined to gain Pappoús's attention.

Kostas Pangalos had become Lissa's guardian after her parents had died when she was a child, but he had been too wrapped up in running his hotel business to have time for his orphaned and traumatised youngest granddaughter. He had died sixteen months ago and had left Eleanor, his favourite grandchild, in charge of Gilpin Leisure.

That final snub from her grandfather had been

a bitter blow for Lissa, and her brother, Mark, had been furious at being overlooked. Eleanor had appointed him as manager of the Pangalos Beach Resort, but Mark was struggling with his own demons and he'd left the hotel's finances in a perilous state before Jace had come along with a rescue package.

Lissa tore her gaze from Takis's mesmerising face and stepped past him. 'My brother-in-law is not responsible for me, and you are certainly not. I'll make my own way to the Pangalos.'

'Stop acting like a spoiled brat. Cancel your taxi and be ready to leave in five minutes.'

'You are unbelievably arrogant,' she snapped.

He did not deny it. His eyes were fixed on her face, and Lissa held her breath when he ran his finger lightly down her cheek. 'You are unbelievably beautiful. But you must know that.' His voice had deepened and rasped like rough velvet across her skin. 'I recognised you from TV adverts and photos in magazines when you were a model for that famous beauty company.'

His face was so close to hers that she could feel his warm breath on her cheek. Her heart missed a beat as he stared at her with smouldering intensity in his eyes. Lissa understood that look. Desire.

Ever since she'd reached puberty and her slender, gymnast's body had developed curves, men had wanted her. At first she had felt uncomfortable, but she'd discovered that the way she looked attracted male admiration, and it had been a heady feeling of power after she had been ignored by her grandfather. But although she had flirted with her admirers, she had never allowed or wanted things to go further.

The attention Takis was showing her filled her with trepidation as well as excitement. He was out of her league. Her brain urged her to step away from him as she would have done if he had been any other man. But there was something about Takis that made her want to respond to the sexual chemistry between them that was almost tangible.

He fascinated her in a way that no other man had ever done and made her wish she could throw off her inhibitions and insecurities. She wondered what it would be like to be kissed by him and was shocked to realise that she longed to find out.

His eyes glittered, and Lissa's heart gave a jolt at the idea that he had read her thoughts. He slowly lowered his face towards her, and she held her breath, mesmerised by his sensual mouth. Unconsciously, she ran her tongue over her bottom lip. Takis stiffened and jerked his head away from her, leaving her torn between relief and disappointment.

'Go and collect your things,' he said in a voice that suggested he was unaffected by the electricity that had crackled between them. It probably happened to him every time he met a woman, Lissa thought ruefully.

But her heart was still thumping after he had nearly kissed her. Why had he changed his mind? Even more puzzling was why she had hoped he would kiss her. She did not know him, and she definitely did not like him. His commanding personality and rampant sex appeal were too much of a threat to her equilibrium.

She was about to insist that she did not want a lift to Sithonia, but the inflexibility in his hard expression warned her that this was a man who always got his own way. It occurred to her that her sister might have asked Jace to arrange for Takis to drive her back to the hotel at the Pangalos Resort. Eleanor had always been protective.

Lissa realised that she had no option but to accept Takis's offer of a lift. She muttered something unladylike as she marched across the lawn towards the house and ground her teeth when his laughter followed her.

CHAPTER TWO

TAKIS HAD MET Lissa's type before. Self-obsessed and with a sense of entitlement that he found irritating. He had assumed he was immune to the feminine wiles of a pretty blonde, especially as his preference was for elegant career women who accepted the limitations of an affair with a man for whom commitment was a no-go area of discussion.

But Lissa was not merely pretty. He sent a sideways glance at her sitting next to him in the car. She was beautiful. Stunningly, breathtakingly beautiful. It was easy to see why the camera loved her exquisite bone structure, the high cheekbones, perfectly symmetrical features and wide eyes that were intensely blue and reminded Takis of the blue-domed churches on Santorini.

Before the wedding, Jace had been impatient for his bride to arrive, but Takis's gaze had swerved from Eleanor in her wedding finery to her bridesmaid wearing a cornflower-blue silk dress that moulded her slender figure and small, high breasts.

He had been unprepared for the impact of Lissa's smile, which held an unexpected sweetness and a vulnerability he told himself he must have imagined. Not so long ago, Lissa had dominated social media sites, and the tabloids had been obsessed with her racy lifestyle, although recently she had not been in the public eye.

During the reception Takis had been lured by the sweet melody of her voice while she'd chatted to him about her life, which seemed to be one long round of parties, he thought cynically. Inexplicably, the sound of her laughter had evoked an ache in his chest. He could not remember a time when he had laughed and not immediately felt guilty.

And he'd had to remind himself of the stories he'd read about Lissa's numerous liaisons with male celebrities who were as famous and as pointless as she was. There had also been rumours of recreational drug-taking, which she'd denied, but it had been reported by various sources that she'd been dropped by the beauty company she had represented. Lissa was trouble with a capital *T*, and he had only agreed to Jace's request to drive her to the Pangalos hotel because it would have been churlish to refuse.

Who was he kidding? Takis mocked himself. He had been unbearably tempted to kiss her when he'd found her in the garden. Thankfully at the last second his brain had overruled his libido, but it had taken every bit of his willpower to resist Lissa's lush mouth. Sexual attraction had sizzled between them and the truth was that he had seized the chance to spend some time with her on the journey to Sithonia.

He glanced at her again and saw that she was holding up a small mirror in one hand and a tube of lipstick in the other. Takis felt a tightening in his groin as he watched her slide the lipstick over her lips, outlining their sensual shape. His mind flashed back to when he was sixteen and living in his father's house in the remote mountain village in northern Greece where he had been born.

Takis knew when he stepped into the kitchen that Spiros was out, probably drunk and brawling in a bar. The tensions at home evaporated when his father was not there.

His stepmother was peering into the cracked mirror over the sink as she painted her mouth with lipstick. He leaned against the door frame and watched Marina. His gaze was riveted on her glossy lips and he felt embarrassed that he could not control the hardness beneath his jeans. His eyes met hers in the mirror and he felt an illicit thrill of desire.

Marina was only a few years older than him. And not technically his stepmother as his father had never married her, even though she had given Spiros another son. It was whispered in the village that Giannis was a bástardos, *but people were careful not to say so in front of Takis, who loved his little half-brother fiercely.*

Marina spun round from the mirror. 'Do you like my lipstick?'

He stared at her scarlet lips, and powerful, urgent feelings throbbed inside him. 'Yes.'

'You want to kiss me, don't you?' Her hips swayed as she walked across the room. She stood so close to him that her breasts pressed against his chest, and he almost forgot to breathe. 'I know you are planning to go away from here. Take me and Giannis with you, and every night you can do more than kiss me. You can have me, Takis.' She brushed her tantalising red lips over his. 'Help me escape from this godforsaken village and your father, and I'll make a man of you.'

Takis had been powerless to resist his stepmother's advances. Helplessly caught up in his teenage crush on her. He could not have predicted that his actions would have diabolical consequences for her and Giannis...

He swallowed hard and forced his mind away from the past and the little boy who would be a man now, had he lived. The memories were too painful and his guilt too great a burden. Something inside him had died with Giannis, and Takis had vowed on the day his brother had been buried that he would never again lose control of his emotions. For nearly twenty years he had found it easy to keep his pledge, and in truth he'd never met a woman who had tempted him to break it.

'You have missed the road where we are meant to

turn off.' Lissa's voice jolted Takis from his thoughts and he cursed beneath his breath as he braked and turned the car around.

'You're very quiet,' he drawled once they were heading in the right direction. Lissa's chatter about people he'd never met and had no interest in would be better than wallowing in the black pit of his past. 'Have you run out of things to say?'

'I talked about myself quite enough at the reception,' she said with a rueful smile that had a peculiar effect on his heart rate. 'It's your turn to tell me about yourself.'

'What do you want to know?'

'Are you married?'

He laughed despite himself. 'Subtlety is not your strong point. I'm not married, and I have no plans to marry, ever.'

'Surely you will get married when you have children?'

'I do not want children. The responsibility of fatherhood holds no appeal for me.' Takis kept his eyes on the road but he sensed that Lissa gave him a curious look.

'I thought all Greek men hope for an heir to continue their family name.'

'Not me. I am the only living descendant of my father.' His fingers involuntarily clenched around the steering wheel as he pictured the heartbreakingly small coffin that had contained his brother's body. 'It is my intention that there will be none after me to carry the name Samaras.'

'Is your father dead?'

'Yes.'

'What about your mum?'

'She died a few years ago.' He had paid for his mother's funeral when he'd been informed of her death by the man she'd been living with. But Takis had not attended to pay his respects because he'd felt nothing for the woman who had abandoned him before he'd been old enough to go to school. *Like he had abandoned Giannis.* Guilt tasted like bitter bile in his throat.

'My parents are both dead too. They died when I was a child, and me and my brother and sister went to live with my grandparents. Nana Francine died not long after. She was heartbroken at losing Mum. I think my grandfather resented the responsibility of bringing up three children.'

'I have heard that Kostas Pangalos was a formidable character.'

'Pappoús was a bully,' Lissa said flatly. 'He made a fuss of Eleanor because she reminded him of our mother, but he didn't care about Mark or me.'

There was a faint tremor in her voice and Takis sensed that she had been hurt by her grandfather's rejection. He could not help feeling sympathy for the little girl who had suffered the devastating loss of both her parents and had felt unloved by her grandfather. He knew what it was like to grow up without love.

He frowned, acknowledging that Lissa was not what he had expected. According to the various online platforms that had been obsessed with her latest hairstyle and the clothes she wore, she was as hard as nails, a beautiful heartbreaker and rampant social climber. Out of the corner of his eye he saw her run her fingers through the jaw-length blonde hair that framed her striking features. *Theos!* She was insanely beautiful.

He forced his attention back on the road. At the wedding reception, men had watched her. Takis had noticed the leering looks they'd given her, as if she were somehow public property, and he'd felt furious and inexplicably possessive.

His turned his head towards her once more and his gaze collided with her deep blue eyes. She hastily looked away and he was intrigued by the blush that stained her cheeks. Her air of innocence had to be an act, but for what purpose? he mused. It was wasted on him. He knew all the manipulations and the games that women liked to play.

'You said that you have known my brother-in-law for some time.' Lissa broke the tense silence that filled the car.

'We met while we were working as labourers on a building site. I had no family, and Jace took care of his mother after his father died. We were both desperate to earn money, but we were teenagers and lied about our age so that the site foreman would employ us.'

The weeks and months after he had left his village had been tough. He had been homeless, penniless and half-mad with grief at the loss of his brother. Jace's friendship had saved him from sinking further into a dark place, Takis acknowledged silently.

'Jace and I supported each other as we developed our careers,' he told Lissa. 'Fate lent a hand when we were lucky enough to share a substantial prize on a lottery ticket. The money allowed Jace to set up his property development company, and I established Perseus, my hospitality and leisure business.'

'Perseus is a character in Greek mythology, isn't he?'

'Yes, he was the slayer of monsters.'

'It seems an odd name for your hotel business. You could have had Zeus, the King of Olympus. Or Hephaestus, the Master of Construction, as you once worked on construction projects.'

Takis silently owned to feeling surprised. 'Have you studied Greek mythology?'

'Not formally, but I'm fascinated by ancient Greek history and I've read a lot of books about it. The Acropolis Museum and the Parthenon are on my wish list of places to visit. Have you been there?'

'No,' Takis admitted. His apartment in Athens overlooked Greece's most famous heritage sites, but he rarely took time off work for leisure pursuits.

He had no intention of explaining that he'd chosen

Perseus, the monster slayer, as a constant reminder of the monster who had lurked inside his father, and perhaps resided within him too.

Spiros had become violent when he'd lost his temper and Takis had endured many beatings from him. He did not know if his father's behaviour was the result of a genetic mutation or if it could be passed down from one generation to the next. But Takis was not prepared to take the risk of having a child of his own. The world would be a better place when his bloodline died with him.

Without a family, or any emotional ties, he had single-mindedly set about making his fortune. He'd been hungry for success, determined never to return to the village close to Greece's border with Albania. The region was blighted by poverty and unemployment and his father had scraped a living by rearing goats—the only livestock suited to the rugged landscape. But life as a goat herder had held no appeal for Takis.

Giannis's death had left a void in his heart, but he'd discovered that his lack of emotions allowed him to be hugely successful in his business dealings. Taking risks did not scare him when he'd already lost the only person he had loved. He'd earned a reputation for ruthlessness as he'd built his empire. From the outside he appeared to have it all. Money, several homes around the world and a constant stream of beautiful women in his bed. But it all felt meaningless. His success meant nothing to him when he carried a secret so dark and shameful that he had never spoken of it to anyone.

Takis mentally shoved his memories back into a box labelled *Do not open.* 'The first hotel I bought in Mykonos was in a bad state of repair. I developed it into an award-winning, five-star hotel, and I own four other luxury leisure complexes located in the Cyclades islands, as well as two high-end hotels in Athens.'

He frowned when he heard a tiny snore and glanced at Lissa. Evidently she had been unimpressed by his achievements for she was fast asleep. He grimaced. Evidently, the only subject that Lissa Buchanan was interested in was herself.

The Pangalos Beach Resort was up ahead now. He turned on to the driveway lined with tall cypress trees and parked the car next to the flight of steps leading up to the main entrance. Light from an overhead lamp streamed through the car window and highlighted Lissa's exquisite features.

Her sideswept fringe had fallen across her face, and Takis had to restrain himself from reaching out to brush her hair off her cheek. Her long, spidery, black eyelashes flew open and her gaze locked on his. The shadows disguised the blue of her eyes, but he saw her pupils dilate and heard her breathing quicken—or was it his own breaths that were unsteady?

Takis swore silently. He did not want to feel so aroused that his erection strained beneath his trousers. He could not remember being so profoundly affected by a woman—except for one woman a long time ago when he had been young and fired up with testosterone. His stepmother had taken advantage of his feelings for her. He had longed for tenderness and affection, but Marina had seen him as a means of escaping her life with his father.

Lissa blinked and Takis sat back in his seat as she came fully awake. 'Sorry.' She yawned. 'I remember you were talking and then I must have nodded off. Did I miss anything?'

'I apologise for boring you with my life story,' he said drily.

'Oh, I always fall asleep on car journeys.' She sat upright and shook her head so that her baby-fine hair swirled around her jaw, drawing his attention to her slender neck. The atmosphere inside the car was combustible, sexual tension lacing the air, and Takis was sure she must be aware of the intense attraction between them.

He was relieved when Lissa opened the door and climbed out of the car. He did the same, but when he followed her across the gravel driveway she stumbled and would have fallen if he had not shot his arm out and caught her.

'Ow! My ankle.'

He helped her over to a low wall so that she could sit down and hunkered in front of her as she rubbed her ankle. 'Why do women wear ridiculous shoes?'

he asked impatiently, inspecting her high-heeled sandals.

'I love my heels. I'm too short without them.'

'You had better take your shoes off in case your ankle swells.'

He watched her unfasten the delicate straps and slide the impractical sandals off. She gave a deep sigh as she wriggled her toes.

'Can you manage to walk?' He straightened up and tore his eyes from her cute toes with the nails painted in sparkly pink varnish.

'I'm sure I can.' She stood up carefully, but when she tried to bear weight on her injured ankle she gave a yelp and sat back down. 'I'll stay here for a bit. The pain will probably go in a few minutes.' She tilted her head and looked up at him. 'Thanks for the lift.'

Takis exhaled slowly. 'I can't leave you out here. I'll carry you into the hotel.'

'There's really no need.'

He ignored her protest and leaned down to scoop her into his arms. She weighed next to nothing, and he was struck by how fragile her slender figure felt beneath her silk dress as he held her against his chest.

'Put your arms around my neck,' he ordered, puzzled by the tension he could feel in her body. She was behaving as if she had not been this close to a man before. An idea he immediately dismissed when he reminded himself of the tabloid stories about her energetic love life with interchangeable boyfriends.

'There is an entrance to the private apartment at the back of the hotel,' Lissa told him as he was about to walk up the front steps of the hotel.

Following her directions, Takis came to a door in a secluded courtyard and waited while she retrieved a key from her purse and gave it to him. He inserted the key in the lock, shouldered the door open and stepped into a hallway where a lift took them to the top floor and directly into the apartment.

He carried Lissa into an airy sitting room and glanced around curiously, aware that Jace had lived in the apartment when he was a boy and his parents had part-owned the hotel, until Kostas Pangalos had conned Dimitri Zagorakis out of his rightful share of the business.

Takis deposited Lissa on the sofa and had every intention of bidding her goodnight and leaving. Except that his body refused to obey his brain. He stared down at her as she leaned back against the cushions. Her hair framed her face like a pale golden bell, and her eyes were astonishingly blue, while her glossy, red mouth promised carnal delights that sent a throb of desire through him. She threatened his self-control more than any other woman had done.

'Would you like a drink? My brother left a bottle of whisky behind when he left.' Lissa stood hesitantly then walked across the room without any sign of discomfort. 'Or there is some brandy,' she said as she opened a cabinet and inspected the contents, 'but it has probably been here some time. My grandfather used to drink brandy. What do you prefer?'

'I don't want a drink. I see that your sprained ankle has miraculously recovered,' he said sardonically.

She shrugged. 'The pain has worn off. When I was younger I used to compete in gymnastics competitions. I fractured my ankle during a routine, and it still twinges occasionally.'

'Are you sure you did not pretend to injure your ankle to lure me into your apartment?'

'Of course not. Why would I?' Lissa sounded genuinely surprised. But she was as changeable as a chameleon, Takis thought grimly. He was bored with playing games. Did she really not feel this desire between them? He stepped closer to her and saw her eyes widen, the pupils dilating.

'Because of this,' he said thickly. His heart was banging against his ribs. He had to kiss her. He wanted to taste those lush, red lips that pouted prettily at him. But he was in control, he assured himself as he slid his arm around her waist.

She gave a soft gasp but did not pull away from him. Her tongue darted over her lips in an unconscious— or was it a deliberate?—invitation.

Lissa had captivated him from the moment he'd seen her at his best friend's wedding, and with a low groan Takis hauled her against him.

CHAPTER THREE

THIS TIME HE was actually going to kiss her. Lissa saw the intent in Takis's eyes as he tightened his arm around her, bringing her body into even closer contact with his. She was conscious of his hard thigh muscles and the solid wall of his chest. She heard the unsteadiness of his breaths and found that she could hardly breathe at all.

She had wondered what it would be like to be kissed by him. To experience his wickedly sexy mouth sliding over hers. And now the fantasy was about to become reality. Her heart clattered against her ribcage. She could not allow a stranger to kiss her. It was crazy and so out of character for her. But he did not feel like a stranger. Takis had fascinated her the instant she'd seen him at her sister's wedding, and even though her brain advised caution it was outvoted by the torrent of desire that swept through her. She sagged against him and tilted her face up to his.

Takis made a low noise in his throat and brushed

his mouth over hers. Once, and then again, taking little sips as he teased her lips apart with the tip of his tongue. Lissa's senses were assailed by his evocative scent, sandalwood cologne and something earthier and male that was uniquely him. She could hear her blood thundering in her ears and felt the hard thud of his heart beneath her hand when she laid it on his chest.

With a soft sigh she parted her lips and capitulated to his sensual demands. His kiss was beyond anything she had imagined in her virginal daydreams. It was not the first time she had been kissed. But she had not had anywhere near the number of boyfriends as had been reported in the gossip columns. She had cultivated a party girl reputation to rebel against her grandfather, who had cared so little about her, but the truth was that at twenty-three she was embarrassed by her inexperience.

Takis pulled her even closer, making her aware of his powerfully muscular physique. His hands felt cool through her silk dress and yet left a trail of fire across her skin as he feathered his fingers down her spine and then clamped hold of her hip to pull her against his hard thighs. His other hand shaped her jaw, angling her mouth so that he could deepen the kiss. His lips were firm and masterful, and she melted in his fire. He had awoken her desire, which had been dormant since she was seventeen, when her first boyfriend had cruelly destroyed her trust along with her reputation.

Lissa did not want to think about him. She kissed Takis unguardedly, parting her lips beneath the pressure of his, and then tentatively dipped her tongue into his mouth. He made a feral noise like the growl of a wolf, and she felt empowered by the realisation that this impossibly gorgeous man desired her. At last he lifted his mouth from hers, but only so that he could trail kisses over her jaw and cheek. His beard felt abrasive against her skin and when he gently nipped her earlobe with his teeth, a shiver ran through her and she pressed herself closer to his hard body.

'*Thélo na se do,*' Takis muttered. Lissa wondered if he was aware that she spoke Greek. Pappoús had insisted that his grandchildren learn the language of his birth. She knew Takis had said, *I want to see you.*

The implication of his words shattered the sensual spell he had cast over her. She tensed when he moved his hand to her nape and tugged the ribbon of her halter-neck dress. In the past, photographs of her wearing a skimpy bikini had appeared in the tabloids, but she had never taken her top off in front of anyone, except for that one shameful incident when she'd been seventeen. The memory made her go cold, and common sense replaced the fire in her blood.

'No.' She pulled free from Takis's arms and quickly retied the straps at the back of her dress. 'I... I can't,' she said huskily. 'We need to stop.'

His eyes narrowed, but he dropped his hands to

his sides and made no move towards her. 'Why?' he demanded, frustration evident in his curt voice.

'We only met for the first time today.' A part of her wanted to give in to the wild feelings Takis had aroused in her, to throw caution to the wind and return to his arms. But he was moving too fast. 'I just think we should slow things down a bit instead of rushing into a relationship.'

Takis's dark brows shot up. 'What kind of relationship were you thinking of? If you were hoping for a grand romance I must disappoint you. But I was under the impression that we both want the same thing.'

'And what is that?' She was chilled by his cool tone.

'To spend the night together.' He frowned when she made a choked sound of denial. 'You flirted with me at the wedding and reception, *koúkla mou*.'

'I am not your *doll*. Maybe I did flirt a little. You are very attractive.' She knew she was blushing and wished she were more experienced. 'It was harmless fun. I didn't expect you to kiss me…and for things to get out of hand.'

His grey eyes were as hard as tensile steel. 'You were throwing out signals that you wanted to sleep with me.'

'I certainly was not.' She glared at him, as furious as Takis clearly was. Her conscience pricked that she had responded eagerly to him. His kiss had been a revelation, but while she had been discovering her hitherto unknown sensuality, Takis believed that she had been leading him on.

'I think you should leave,' she said shakily.

'I agree.' He strode across the room and paused with his hand on the door handle, turning his head to give her a glowering look. 'Do you get a kick out of teasing and tantalising a man?' he said contemptuously.

She drew a sharp breath. 'I have the right to say no.'

'Of course.' He roamed his eyes over her flushed face and lower to the betraying hard points of her nipples jutting beneath her dress. 'Perhaps you do not know what you want, *koúkla mou*.'

'Perhaps not,' she said in a low voice. 'I've never done anything like this before.'

'What do you mean?'

Lissa let out her breath slowly. 'The truth is that I'm a virgin.'

Takis stared at her in silence for a few seconds and then he laughed. It was not a pleasant laugh, and it grated on Lissa's fraught emotions. 'How do you explain the stories in the media, detailing your affairs with idiotic young men who crave fame and adulation as much as you do?' he demanded.

She flushed and said defensively, 'Everyone knows that the tabloids depend on scandalous stories to sell more copies. Most of the stuff they print is made up or exaggerated.'

'It is you who is a fantasist if you think you can convince me that you are as pure as snow.'

'Isn't that a case of double standards?' she demanded. 'It's okay for a man to have a playboy reputation, but a woman is a slut.'

'I certainly do not believe that. Women are entitled to a sex life as much as men. But the point I was making is that you are claiming to be a sexual innocent when the evidence is to the contrary.' He swept his icy gaze over her. 'You might play games with other men, but don't try to play them with me.'

'Get out,' she snapped, goaded beyond endurance.

'Don't worry, I'm going.'

He went without another word, but the loud slam of the door behind him spoke volumes. Good riddance, Lissa told herself. He was arrogant beyond belief and she hoped she never saw him again. But her traitorous body did not share the sentiment and she ached with sexual frustration that she'd never experienced before, as well as an inexplicable sense of hurt.

She walked listlessly into the bathroom to remove her make-up before moving into the bedroom where she stripped off her dress and donned a distinctly unsexy nightshirt with a picture of kittens printed on the front.

Damn Takis Samaras, she thought angrily as she climbed into bed and pummelled the pillows into submission. Why on earth had she blurted out to him that was a virgin? She had never confessed the truth to anyone else, not even her sister. She felt humiliated by Takis's refusal to believe her and angry with herself for confiding in him.

As she was about to switch off the lamp, Lissa remembered to take her medication. Eighteen months ago she had been diagnosed with an overactive thyroid and been prescribed tablets to adjust her thyroid levels. Thankfully, the worst symptoms of hyperthyroidism—weight loss, exhaustion and feeling nervous and agitated—were now under control.

At the time that she had become ill, the tabloids had alleged she was addicted to class A drugs. The story had gained credence when she had been photographed looking painfully thin and drawn, stumbling out of a nightclub. Had Takis seen *those* photos and assumed that she was the party girl portrayed in certain sections of the media?

It might explain his behaviour, although it did not excuse it, she thought grimly. The best thing to do was to try to get some sleep and forget about Takis. But when she closed her eyes, she pictured his brutally handsome face. The taste of him was still on her lips and there was a heavy sense of regret in her heart.

Regret for kissing him. Regret for asking him to stop.

Takis glanced moodily around the packed ballroom where women in brightly coloured dresses flitted like butterflies and men wearing dinner suits resembled penguins. The charity fundraising ball for the Zagorakis Foundation was hosted every year by Jace in Thessaloniki, but this year the venue had been changed to the Pangalos hotel. Takis had cited work commitments as an excuse to stay away. Yet here he was, nursing a stiff Scotch in one hand while he scanned the crowd for Lissa's distinctive platinum-blonde bob.

He could not rationalise to himself why he had changed his mind and decided to attend the party. The hotel evoked unwelcome memories of his previous visit when he'd carried Lissa up to the private apartment where she had stayed after Jace and Eleanor's wedding. For the past month, Takis had tried unsuccessfully to forget the one woman who his instincts warned him to avoid. But his mind kept replaying those moments when he had taken Lissa in his arms and covered her lush, red lips with his mouth.

Her passionate response had fuelled his desire like a flame to tinder. But then she had pulled back and he'd glimpsed uncertainty in her eyes, a wariness that had puzzled him until he'd reminded himself that she was no doubt playing a manipulative game. He had rejected the idea that her air of innocence could be real when everything else told him it was a lie. Her accusation of double standards was not true. He did not care how many lovers she'd had, but he put a high value on honesty.

He'd stormed out of Lissa's apartment in a furious mood made worse by the nagging ache in his groin. But his anger had been as much with himself as with her. He did not understand why he had come on to her so strongly, or why he'd reacted so badly when she'd rejected him. He'd never had a problem if a woman had said no to him in the past, although it did not happen very often, he acknowledged wryly. He was ashamed that when Lissa had called a halt to their passion he'd reacted like a hormonal adolescent. She made him feel out of control and he knew how dangerous that could be.

Takis's thoughts turned to himself as that teenage boy on the cusp of manhood, his body a riot of hormones and his heart craving love that his parents had never given him…

Marina wound her arms around his neck and tugged his mouth down closer to hers. 'I bet you've never kissed a woman before. Shall I show you how it's done?'

Takis swallowed hard. His youthful body was so aroused it hurt, but although he hated his father, he felt some loyalty to Spiros. 'You are my father's woman,' he muttered.

She laughed softly. 'One kiss won't hurt.'

He looked into her dark eyes and felt a rush of emotions as he clumsily pressed his mouth to her lips. His body shook when she parted her lips beneath his. He kissed Marina with all the love in his lonely heart. But there came the sound of heavy foot-

steps in the hallway, warning him that his father had returned to the house.

Takis hastily stepped away from his stepmother, but she grabbed hold of his arm. 'Promise that you will take me and Giannis away with you or I will tell Spiros that you kissed me,' she hissed.

'If you do, he will kill me.' Takis had suffered his father's violent temper many times.

Marina shrugged. 'You had better start making plans for us to leave.'

The truth had soon become clear to Takis. Marina had manipulated him for her own purpose. In that moment she had shattered his youthful, trusting heart and he'd learned the painful lesson that love was for fools. He had crept out of the house the same night, determined to escape his stepmother's machinations. Days later, he'd learned that his father, Marina and Giannis had all died when a fire had raged through the house.

Takis had not mourned Spiros. He had felt some guilt that he'd refused to help Marina get away from his father. But far more devastating had been the realisation that he had abandoned his little brother to a terrible fate. If only he had stayed he would have saved Giannis from the inferno or died trying.

Takis took a swig of whisky and forced his mind away from the memories that would haunt him forever. In the ballroom, the ongoing battle between the disco music and the white noise of countless conversations was a welcome distraction. He caught sight of Jace and Eleanor dancing close together. The tender expression on his best friend's face as he looked at his wife startled Takis. He had assumed that Jace's marriage was a business arrangement that would allow him to claim back his family's share of the Pangalos hotel. But from what Takis could see, Jace appeared to be captivated by his fair and gentle Eleanor.

As for that sister of hers… His brows snapped together when he thought of Lissa. It irritated him to have to admit that he was disappointed she was not at the ball. He had been certain she would be at the highly prestigious social event. Partying was what Lissa did best, everyone knew that.

Pride had prevented him from asking Eleanor if her sister had remained in England. Jace had mentioned that Lissa worked at Francine's, the hotel in Oxford owned by Gilpin Leisure. Eleanor had inherited the business on her grandfather Kostas Pangalos's death. Jace had also mentioned that Lissa had been prevented by a clause in her grandfather's will from accessing her trust fund until she was twenty-five. Perhaps it was for that reason that Eleanor had employed her sister, Takis mused. He could not imagine flighty Lissa holding down a mundane job as a hotel receptionist.

A commotion over by the doors that led to the terrace caught his attention. An argument had broken

out between two young men and they squared up
to each other until a figure stepped between them.

Lissa.

His heart slammed into his ribs. Why was he
surprised that she was at the centre of trouble and
more than likely the cause of it? His fingers clenched
around his glass as he lifted it to his lips and took
another gulp of whisky. Every muscle and sinew in
his body was taut and he could hear the hard thud
of his pulse in his ears.

Takis told himself that his reaction to Lissa was
no different from that of every other red-blooded
male in the room. Her beauty made her the focus
of attention and tonight she looked stunning in a
sparkly silver sheath dress that moulded her slender
figure. The low-cut gown was strapless and had the
effect of pushing her small breasts high. A side-split
in the long skirt revealed a shapely leg and a tantalising glimpse of a lacy stocking top when she walked.

He moved his eyes back up to her exquisite face,
framed by her blonde hair that flicked against her
jawline. She was his hottest sexual fantasy. He must
have imagined a vulnerability about her when he'd
kissed her. There was no mystery to Lissa Buchanan.
She could bring a man to his knees with a smile on
those lush lips of hers that promised sensual nirvana.

He had to have her, Takis realised. Bedding her
was the solution that would free him from his in-
convenient obsession with her. He beckoned to a
waiter and put his empty glass down on the tray but

declined another drink. His heart was racing, and he did not need alcohol when anticipation surged through his veins like a powerful drug as he strode across the ballroom.

CHAPTER FOUR

LISSA FROZE WHEN she spotted Takis threading a path through the crowd on the dance floor towards her. She had only decided to attend the charity ball after her sister had mentioned that Jace's best friend could not make it. No way did she want to run into the most arrogant man on the planet ever again.

She was having a perfectly nice time at the party, or so she tried to convince herself. Plenty of men had asked her to dance, and she'd drunk champagne, although she had learned from bitter experience to stick to one alcoholic drink, and she could make a glass of fizz last all night. She had laughed and flirted and pretended to be the glamorous socialite everyone believed her to be. Only she knew that the truth was very different.

The evening had felt flat, flatter than usual. Until she saw Takis was here and fireworks exploded inside her.

He halted in front of her. His grey eyes gleamed like polished steel and his chiselled features were utterly mesmerising. Lissa could not look away from him or greet him as coolly as she would if he was any casual acquaintance. Her breath was trapped in her lungs and her mouth had dried.

Takis looked dangerously sexy dressed all in black—an elegant tuxedo, a silk shirt open at the throat and his bow tie hanging loose around his neck as if he had impatiently tugged the two ends apart.

'I didn't think you would be at the ball,' she blurted out, cringing that she appeared so gauche.

'I wrapped up a business meeting quicker than I'd expected and I arrived a few minutes ago. What was all that about?' he drawled. At her puzzled look, he said, 'I suppose the two young colts were fighting over you?'

She blushed because he was so close to the truth. Jean-Claud Delfour's family owned a vast wine estate in the Loire Valley and Tommy Matheson was the son of an American billionaire. They were at the ball as representatives of their families, who had made large donations to the charity that Jace headed. Lissa had met the two young men on the London party circuit.

'They've drunk too much,' she said with a shrug. 'I'm not a piece of meat to be fought over. *I* choose who I want to dance with.'

Takis's gaze dropped to her bare shoulders and his mouth crooked in an enigmatic smile. 'Choose to dance with me.'

It sounded like an order that she had no intention of obeying. But somehow she was standing so close to him that her cheek was against the lapel of his jacket and he slid his arm around her waist. He captured her hand in his and pulled her even closer to his whipcord body.

It had to be then that the DJ swapped the frenetic disco music for a slow jazz number, Lissa thought despairingly. While she danced with Takis she felt as though they were the only two people in the ball-room, in the universe, moving in perfect synchrony to the slow beat of the music. She was fiercely aware of his hard thighs pressed against her, and his hand at the small of her back exerted pressure to bring her pelvis flush with his.

His warm breath fanned her cheek as he murmured, 'You didn't call.'

Lissa remembered the text message she had received from him days after her sister's wedding. She'd left the Pangalos hotel early the next morning to avoid any chance of running into Takis again and had spent several hours at the airport, waiting for her flight to London.

Back in Oxford, she had thrown herself into her job at Francine's hotel, where she had been the general manager since Eleanor had married and moved to Greece. Lissa was grateful to her sister for giving her the chance to work in the family business. It was something she had wanted to do—more to prove that she could rather than a burning desire to be a hotel manager. Her grandfather had accused her of lacking a strong work ethic after he'd seen newspaper pictures of her sunbathing on beaches in exotic locations around the world. Out of stubborn pride she had not told him that she fitted her modelling work around studying for a diploma in hospitality management.

Pappoús had made her feel worthless, but Lissa had hidden her true feelings behind a mask of bravado. Accepting the modelling contract had given her financial freedom. She had pretended to be an irresponsible party girl, partly to annoy her grandfather, but her public image was also a defence to stop anyone discovering that the real Lissa Buchanan felt *lost*.

The text from Takis had flashed on to her phone's screen one evening, and her heart had pounded as she'd reread it countless times. She did not know how he had got hold of her number and wondered if he had asked her sister for it. He had included his own contact details and the message simply read:

It would be good to hear from you.

She tilted her head up to his face and her heart missed a beat when her eyes meshed with his glinting gaze. 'Did you expect me to want to speak to you after you were so vile? You're cute, but not that cute,' she said drily.

His husky laughter rolled through her, and she felt inordinately pleased that she had amused him. She was transfixed by his smile and the flash of white teeth in his darkly tanned face. But it would be unwise to lower her guard against a wolf, however docile he might seem.

'I am definitely not cute like a little puppy dog.' His smile disappeared and the sudden grimness in his voice sent a shiver through Lissa. 'You should keep away from me.'

'Difficult, considering our current position,' she murmured. Her feet momentarily lost the rhythm of the music and Takis tightened his hold on her waist as she stumbled. She did not understand why the bleakness in his voice made her heart ache.

'As a matter of fact, I came to your apartment the morning after we argued to apologise for my behaviour, but the maid said you had already left for the airport.'

'I had an early flight,' she fibbed, smiling at him. Her heart lifted with the knowledge that Takis regretted the unpleasant way the evening of the wedding had ended as much as she had. She was willing to put it behind them and move on. But move on to what exactly? She did not know what Takis wanted from her, although the hungry gleam in his eyes gave her a fair idea. She could not ignore their white-hot sexual chemistry, but was she brave enough to throw herself into the flames?

Perhaps he had the ability to read her mind. He drew her even closer to him, and desire tugged in the pit of her stomach when she felt the hard proof of his arousal beneath his trousers. 'Shall we start over?' he suggested.

Her breath caught in her throat. He fascinated her more than any man had ever done. 'I'd like that,' she said shyly.

A frown briefly appeared on Takis's hard-boned face, but then he smiled, although the expression in his eyes remained speculative. And all the while they danced hip to hip. Lissa's breasts were crushed against his chest and the fire inside her burned hotter, wilder, out of control. Takis muttered something beneath his breath as he swept her across the ballroom and out of the door on to the terrace. A few guests were standing around chatting and he steered Lissa over to an empty corner.

'Are you staying in the private apartment here at the hotel?'

'Jace's mother and her nurse are using the apartment, and I have a room in the staff quarters.' Lissa sighed. 'My room is the size of a broom cupboard and has a view of the car park. But I made a last-minute decision to attend the ball and the hotel was fully booked.'

'I am in the penthouse suite, which has a private roof terrace and a pool where guests can swim naked beneath the stars if they so desire,' he drawled.

Lissa's mind ran riot as she imagined him naked. She had been acutely aware of his muscular body beneath his suit while they had been dancing. She wondered if Takis had chosen his words deliberately to seduce her. To let her know what would happen if she gave in to the desire coursing though her.

The answer blazed in his eyes, and her heart skittered. After their last disastrous meeting she had tried to convince herself that she disliked him, that she should forget him, but she had failed on both counts, she acknowledged with a sigh.

Her tongue darted across her lips. 'Do you desire?' she whispered. 'To swim beneath the stars, I mean.'

'I do.' The dark intensity of his voice set every nerve ending on Lissa's skin alight. 'Would you like to swim with me?'

Her pulse was racing so fast that she felt dizzy, unmoored and uncharacteristically reckless. She had the sense that she was standing at the top of a precipice and about to leap into the unknown. 'Yes,' she whispered.

Takis caught hold of her hand and lifted it up to his mouth. He grazed his lips over her knuckles and Lissa felt a sensation like an electrical current shoot up her arm. She watched his dark head descend and anticipation ran through her as he angled his mouth over hers. She wanted him to kiss her, there was no point denying it to herself.

She parted her lips and glimpsed a fierce gleam in his eyes as he claimed her mouth with arrogant possession. His kiss was even better than she remembered, hotter and more intense, and she melted against him, helpless to resist his passionate demands.

All her adult life Lissa had refused to be the kind of woman she had allowed her grandfather to think she was. She had hugged the secret of her virtue to herself when Pappoús had criticised her after reading reports of her wild lifestyle. But Kostas was dead, and Lissa could barely remember why she'd engaged in a stupid battle of wills with him. She no longer had to be in awe of an old man who had disapproved of her. She could do whatever she wanted.

Takis's warm breath filled her mouth and his raw, male scent intensified her longing. He broke off the kiss at last and stared intently at her, his expression half-hidden in the shadows. And then he tilted his head back and looked up at the dark sky, studded with diamonds.

'It is a perfect night for swimming beneath the stars, *koúkla mou*.' He held out his hand, and after an imperceptible hesitation Lissa linked her fingers through his.

Takis ushered Lissa into his penthouse suite, and as she heard the door close with a soft snick she was beset with doubts. When they had left the ballroom and entered a lift, there had been other guests besides them. But now she was alone with the most enigmatic and sinfully attractive man she'd ever met. And somewhere on the way up to his hotel suite the reality of what she was doing had sunk in and her confidence had deserted her.

'Would you like a drink?'

It was tempting to settle her nerves with alcohol, but the one and only time she had been drunk had ended with her very public humiliation.

'No, thank you,' she said stiffly. She was aware that she sounded like a teenager on a first date, and the truth was that she had never really moved on from the deeply upsetting incident when she'd been seventeen.

Takis's eyes narrowed when she stepped away from him, but he made no attempt to touch her. Lissa reminded herself that she had been alone with him in her apartment the previous time they had both stayed at the Pangalos hotel. But tonight was different. She had responded to his passionate kiss and encouraged him to have expectations that, though she'd desperately wanted to, she hadn't been sure she could deliver.

'I don't usually do this,' she told him in a low voice. 'Go to a hotel room with a man I barely know, I mean.'

'No?' His tone was sardonic.

Lissa bit her lip, feeling at a loss to know how to explain that she was not the person he believed her to be. That she had courted scandal and lived up to her party girl reputation to provoke her grandfather, but that she was now ashamed of her childish attempts to gain Pappoús's attention.

Takis shrugged. 'You came here of your own free will and there is nothing to prevent you from leaving. No chains across the door.' He strode across the room towards the glass doors that slid open smoothly when he flicked a switch on the wall. 'I'm going for a swim. Join me, if you wish,' he drawled as he stepped outside.

The only chains were in her mind, Lissa realised.

She looked over at the front door of the penthouse and felt a hollow sensation inside at the thought of walking away from Takis without exploring the powerful chemistry they shared. Did she have the courage to overcome her inhibitions and behave like any other single, twenty-three-year-old woman? There was only one way to find out.

The sound of a faint splash from outside drew her over to the glass doors. Light from the penthouse spilled on to the terrace, but the pool was dark and Takis was a shadowy figure cutting through the water. He swam several lengths before he stopped and hauled himself half out of the pool, resting his elbows on the tiles.

'So you've decided to stay.' Nothing in his tone gave an indication of his thoughts.

'Yes.' Trying to ignore the frantic thud of her heart, Lissa walked across the terrace, her stiletto heels clipping against the tiles. 'But I don't have a swimsuit.'

Takis grinned. 'Neither do I.' He heaved himself out of the pool with a lithe movement and stood a little way off from her. Water streamed down his body, running in rivulets over his broad chest and washboard-flat abdomen.

Lissa's gaze followed the tracks of water down to his black boxers that sat low on his hips, and she felt relieved and just the tiniest bit disappointed that he wasn't completely naked. A partially clothed Takis was enough for her to cope with. At the ball he'd looked magnificent in a tuxedo, but the sight of his bare chest with a smattering of dark hair that arrowed down to the waistband of his boxers set her pulse hammering. He was so *male*, so virile and potent, and she felt intensely aware of her softer, feminine body.

'Presumably you are wearing underwear, which is not so different from a bikini,' he said. 'Do you need me to unzip your dress?'

'I can manage.' She could do this, Lissa told herself. Undoing her dress wasn't a problem as it had a side zip, but undressing in front of Takis tested her resolve to throw off the shackles of her past.

Silver sequins sparkled like tiny stars as the dress slipped to the floor, leaving her in her stockings, stiletto shoes, lacy knickers and strapless bra. She had worn less on the beach, she reminded herself.

Takis uttered a low growl of admiration that caused her nipples to harden. Before her nerve could fail, she kicked off her shoes and peeled her stockings down her legs. 'Which end is the shallow end?' she asked him when she walked towards the pool.

'It's all one depth. I am a couple of inches over six feet and I can stand on the bottom, but I doubt you will be able to as you are much shorter than me. I left the underwater lights off so that we can swim by starlight.'

Lissa stared down at the dark depths of the pool and her stomach muscles clenched with fear. Why on earth had she thought that this was a good idea? 'I'm not a confident swimmer,' she admitted. 'I don't like being out of my depth in water.' She was way out of her depth with Takis before she'd even dipped a toe in the pool, she thought. Panic made her breathing erratic.

Takis jumped into the pool and disappeared beneath the surface. He reappeared and slicked his wet hair back from his brow. 'I'll stay close to you so that you can grab hold of me if you feel nervous.'

Terrified was a more accurate description. Her phobia of deep water had started when she'd been a child. She stood on the top of the pool steps and was aware of a dryness in her mouth and her rapid heartbeat. She felt an urge to run back into the penthouse. But she could not spend the rest of her life running away from scary situations, Lissa thought, feeling impatient with herself. She wanted to change who she was, and change began with simple steps.

Steeling her nerves, she put her foot on the second rung of the steps and then the third, slowly lowering herself into the pool until her shoulders were beneath the water. She stretched her leg down but could not feel the bottom with her toes. Taking a deep breath, she swam a few strokes, but panic overwhelmed her and she felt herself sinking. She splashed frantically and swallowed a mouthful of water.

'Be calm. I am here.' A pair of strong arms wrapped around her waist.

Lissa clutched Takis's shoulders. 'It's no good. I can't do it. Will you take me back to the side, please?'

'Try to relax,' he murmured. 'Why do you dislike being in a swimming pool so much?'

She thought about giving a flippant excuse that her hairstyle would be ruined if she got it wet. But something in Takis's steady gaze made her want to confide in him.

'My parents drowned when I was ten. They were in Sri Lanka to celebrate their wedding anniversary.' Her voice shook. 'They went away and never came back.'

'That was a terrible tragedy,' he said softly. 'Have you ever sought help to overcome your understandable fear?'

She shook her head. 'I've never told anyone. It sounds silly, but when I'm in the water I imagine how scared Mum must have been when she was caught in a strong sea current and couldn't make it back to the beach. My dad tried to save her, but he was swept away too.'

Takis brushed a strand of hair off her cheek. His eyes were silver-bright in the darkness. 'I promise you won't drown. Will you trust me to keep you safe, *koúkla mou*?'

There was no reason why she should trust him, yet oddly she did. 'Yes,' she whispered.

'You need to build your confidence in the water by learning to float. Try to relax and I will support you while you lie back.'

Lissa attempted to follow his instructions, but when the water filled her ears she panicked and grabbed his arm. 'It's no good. I'm hopeless.' Her grandfather had often told her so, and she'd never had a reason not to believe him.

'Nonsense,' Takis said calmly. 'Can you feel my arm beneath your back? I won't let you sink. Try again,' he encouraged.

Her second attempt was more successful. The sensation of water in her ears made her feel terrified that it would cover her face and she'd be unable to breathe. But she trusted that Takis would not allow her to sink and gradually her muscles unlocked as she discovered that there was no need to thrash her arms and legs frantically in an effort to stay afloat.

After a few minutes Takis dropped his arm away from her so that she was floating on her own. 'Well done,' he said. 'It takes courage to face up to fear. You have taken the first step and I have no doubt that you will become a more confident swimmer.'

Lissa was not used to being praised. More often she had been criticised by her grandfather. She felt a spurt of pride in herself for starting to tackle her fear.

'Thank you for being so patient.' She gave Takis a shy smile and he looked puzzled for a moment before his answering smile set her pulse racing.

He placed his hands on her waist, drawing her towards him and turning her around so that her back rested on his chest and the water lapped around her breasts. 'Look up at the sky,' he bade her.

Lissa tilted her head and caught her breath as she stared at the glittering canopy above them. There was no moon, and the black sky was filled with more stars than she had ever seen. 'It's incredible,' she said in awe. 'I've always lived in a city and never noticed how bright the stars are because of the light pollution.'

'When I was a boy I used to climb the mountain near my home, and when night fell, the stars seemed close enough to touch.'

'That sounds lovely. Is it a pretty place where you grew up?'

He gave a short laugh. 'I have not been back there for twenty years. The scenery attracted a few tourists in the summer, but there was no work or prospects for the people who lived there. I climbed the mountain hoping to see a better place on the other side of it. I couldn't wait to leave.'

Lissa wanted to know more about his past, but his terse tone warned her to curb her curiosity. She stared up at the stunning light show in the sky. Nature at its most glorious. Her senses became attuned to the rhythmic rise and fall of Takis's chest that felt like a wall of steel behind her. His strength made her feel safe and the heat of his body pressed up close to hers was intoxicating.

She let her head drop back a little more so that it rested on his shoulder. The night air was so still that she heard his breathing quicken, and his hands tightened on her waist. Her heart gave a jolt when she felt his body stir beneath his boxers, and the hard proof of his arousal nudged her bottom.

'I'm curious,' he drawled, turning her in his arms so that she was facing him. 'Why did you accept my invitation of a night-time swim when you have a fear of deep water?'

'I didn't think we were actually going to swim,' Lissa admitted. Her heart missed a beat at the glint in his eyes.

'Ah, so was stargazing the attraction?'

She could pretend to agree, but she had been putting on a pretence for much of her life. It was time to be honest with herself and with Takis.

'You are the attraction,' she whispered.

CHAPTER FIVE

'YOU TAKE MY breath away,' Takis said huskily. He pulled Lissa closer to him so that her breasts brushed against his chest. 'Wrap your legs around me,' he instructed as he waded through the water, carrying her over to the edge of the pool.

He lifted her on to the tiled floor and heaved himself out of the water. Catching hold of her hand, he led her over to a circular daybed and drew her into his arms once more. His eyes gleamed in the darkness and the predatory expression on his face once again reminded Lissa of a wolf. A mixture of excitement and faint apprehension sent a shiver through her.

'Are you cold?' He picked up a towel and blotted the moisture from her shoulders, and then ran his finger lightly over her décolletage, down to the edge of her bra. 'Your wet underwear needs to come off,' he murmured.

Lissa looked down and saw that her bra had turned see-through, and her nipples were two dark outlines jutting through the material. Her common sense told her that she should wrap the towel around her and return to the penthouse to change into her dress. But her feet refused to obey her brain and she did not move when Takis reached behind her back and unfastened her bra.

As the flimsy underwear fell away from her breasts, she stiffened, remembering the humiliating events that had followed when she'd allowed her first boyfriend to see her naked breasts. She had been unaware that photographs of her had been taken until they had been made public.

But she reminded herself that she had put her trust in Takis in the pool when he had helped her to overcome her fear of drowning. She released her breath slowly, but at the same time her heart rate accelerated when she saw the expression in his eyes.

'Eísai tóso ómorfos,' he said. 'You are so beautiful,' he repeated in English.

A dull flush spread over his angular face. He lifted his hand and touched the pulse thudding at the base of her throat, and then he lowered his head and pressed his mouth to the same place before feathering kisses along her collarbone.

He lifted his face to hers, and Lissa's lips parted involuntarily as he claimed her mouth in a deeply sensual kiss that lit a fire inside her. The last remnants of her tension eased, and she gave a soft sigh when he slid his hands down from her shoulders and stroked the sides of her breasts.

His fingers drifted over her dainty curves, as if he were learning her shape by touch as well as by sight. She caught her breath when he finally brushed his thumbs across her nipples.

'Do you like that?' he murmured as her nipples hardened beneath his caresses.

'Yes.' His touch was addictive, and she wanted more. Need and longing were emotions she had never felt for any other man, certainly not to this degree. Her teenage crush on Jason had not prepared her for the sweet flood of desire that pooled between her thighs as Takis gently rolled her nipples between his fingers. 'Oh,' she gasped. 'Yes.'

He made a rough sound in his throat that sent a tremor through her. 'Do you have any idea what you do to me?' he rasped. 'I tried to forget you, but I failed.' Frustration was evident in his voice.

'I couldn't forget you either.' Lissa whispered the words against his lips as he kissed her again. He tumbled her down on to the daybed and stretched out beside her, trailing kisses down her neck and over the slopes of her breasts.

She felt his warm breath on her nipple and her heart gave a jolt. She'd never permitted a man to put his mouth on her breasts, but now she silently willed Takis to do just that. He flicked his tongue across one tender peak and then the other, and Lissa could not hold back a sob of delight.

She clutched his shoulders and felt the ripple of powerful muscles beneath her fingertips. The pleasure he wrought with his mouth on her breasts was so intense that she moved her hips restlessly, desperate to assuage the insistent throb *there* at her feminine core.

Takis moved his mouth back up to hers and kissed her with mind-blowing sensuality. He demanded her complete capitulation, and she gave it willingly, sliding one hand into his jet-dark hair, while the other explored the hard line of his jaw, covered with stubble that felt abrasive against her palm.

He took everything she offered and demanded more. His tongue plundered the moist interior of her mouth, eliciting a response that she could not deny him. He draped one heavy thigh across her legs and captured her wrists in his hand, pinning them above her head. And then he put his mouth on her breast and sucked her nipple in a highly erotic caress.

He transferred his attention to her other breast and Lissa was vaguely aware that the thin cries she could hear came from her. But she could not control her reaction, as the pleasure Takis evoked with his hands and mouth on her body drove her mad with longing.

Her breath left her on a shuddering sigh when he tugged her knickers off and pushed her legs apart. She had never been naked with a man before and a tiny voice inside her asked if she was ready to take this next step. The answer had to be, *Yes!* She was a twenty-three-year-old virgin and she wanted to take charge of her life and finally explore her sensuality with this fascinating man.

Takis traced his fingers along her inner thigh, moving inexorably higher. A quiver of anticipation ran through Lissa when he cupped his hand over her feminine mound.

'Relax,' he murmured as he stroked her moist opening. But it was impossible to relax when everything he did was shockingly new. She gasped when he pressed his thumb over the hidden nub of her clitoris. The sensation was indescribable, and she instinctively arched her hips towards his hand.

Takis gave a husky laugh and slipped a finger into her slick wetness. 'Tell me how I can give you pleasure, *koúkla mou.*'

His voice intruded on the sensual spell he had woven around her. The realisation of what she was doing made her heart clatter against her ribs. Takis was kissing her mouth again while he moved his hand in a rhythmic motion. He stretched her a little wider so that he could slip another finger into her molten heat.

It felt so amazingly good when he swirled his fingers inside her. Each movement of his hand drove Lissa higher and her breathing quickened as she felt herself nearing an orgasm. When Takis lifted his head and stared down at her, she could not bring herself to meet his gaze. Not when his fingers were still deep inside her, swirling in an insistent dance that made her quake. She skimmed her hands over his chest, tracing the arrowing of hairs down to his boxer shorts. Through the still-damp material she felt the hard ridge of his arousal push against her hand.

'I want to make love to you, Lissa. Thinking about you has driven me crazy for weeks.' He withdrew his fingers from her trembling body and propped himself up on an elbow, slipping his hand beneath her chin and forcing her to look at him.

'Before we take this any further I need to make something clear.' The sudden coolness in his voice sent a prickle of warning across her skin. 'I'm not looking for a relationship. I want you, but for one night only. That's all I'm offering. One perfect night together.'

She was glad that Takis had been honest, while trying to ignore the sinking feeling in her stomach. She shouldn't feel hurt because he had set parameters and insisted that sex was all he wanted. *Why would he be interested in you as a person or want to get to know you better?* taunted a voice inside her that reminded her of her inadequacy.

'What have you got against relationships?' she asked him.

He shrugged. 'My life is my own. I work hard and play hard and I choose not to have personal commitments. I enjoy sex and I'm good at it.' The heat in his gaze sent a lick of flames down to Lissa's feminine core. 'But sexual ecstasy is simply that,' Takis drawled. 'It has no higher meaning, and it is not a connection between souls. I know this because I do not have a soul.'

She stared at his hard-boned face and sensual mouth that she found utterly fascinating. There was no rational explanation, no right or wrong. She simply wanted to make love with him.

'One perfect night,' she murmured.

His wicked smile stole her breath. 'Do not doubt it,' he said softly as he cradled her cheek in his hand and dipped his head towards her, slanting his mouth over hers.

His kiss blazed through her and she parted her lips, eager to respond to his sensual demands. He lay down beside her and roved his hands over her body, exploring every dip and curve. The scrape of his jaw on her breasts was a sensory delight that made her shiver as he skilfully heightened her anticipation.

Takis pulled off his boxers, freeing his erection, and Lissa drew a swift breath when she felt the hard length of his arousal nudge between her thighs. She wanted to explore his male body, but when she ran her fingers along his shaft, he groaned.

'There's no time for that. I have to have you now,' he rasped. His urgency fuelled her own longing for him to assuage the sweet throb of desire between her thighs, but she was confused when he rolled away from her and reached for his jacket, which he'd left on a chair. Understanding dawned when he took a packet of condoms from the pocket and quickly prepared himself.

He knelt over her and slipped a finger inside her, his eyes glinting like molten silver when he discovered how wet she was. 'You are ready for me, *koúkla mou*.'

Lissa felt a flutter of anticipation as he positioned himself between her legs and slid his hands beneath her bottom. It was actually happening. Takis was about to make love to her. She *was* ready. So hot and needy. His wide shoulders blocked out the light of the stars and she could not see the expression on his face.

'Bend your knees,' he murmured, and when she obeyed, he eased forward and Lissa felt his swollen tip push between her silken folds. She tried to prepare mentally and physically for him to possess her. But then he made a harsh sound in his throat and thrust into her, and it *hurt*, and she snatched a sharp breath.

It was not possible, Takis told himself. He must have imagined that Lissa's body had initially resisted when he'd entered her. He pulled back a little way and stared down at her. An alarm bell rang in his mind when she evaded his gaze, but his eyes were drawn to her lush mouth, reddened from his kisses, and all he could think of was how desperately he wanted to kiss her again.

She was so tight and hot. His brain was sending him a startling message, but he could not comprehend the possibility that she had not done this before. He tried to move and withdraw from her, but it felt like his shaft was being gripped in a velvet glove and he could not fight the tsunami of need that swept through him.

'Am I hurting you?' he bit out. He felt dangerously out of control.

'No…' she whispered slowly. She moved her hips as if trying to find a more comfortable position. The ripples of her internal muscles squeezing his shaft very nearly made Takis come there and then. 'It feels better now,' she said in a small voice that was like a kick in his guts.

He should stop. He would stop. But somehow, instead of pulling out, he sank deeper into her and groaned as every nerve ending on his body thrummed with expectation. He was greedy for more, and when he fought his desire and again pulled back, Lissa clutched his shoulders and arched her hips in mute supplication, and Takis was lost.

He supported his weight on one elbow and slipped his hand between their joined bodies, seeking the tight little bud of her femininity. He caressed her with his fingers and simultaneously set a rhythm, slow at first as he pressed deeper. He withdrew and pressed again, quicker now, each thrust harder than the last as the storm inside him built.

It was elemental and fierce and uncontrollable. With a sense of shock, he realised that he was about to be overwhelmed. He clenched his jaw, but he was no longer the master of his body and he gave a savage groan at the moment of release as pleasure ripped through him.

Takis's chest heaved with the effort of dragging oxygen into his lungs. Deep shudders racked his body and in a distant corner of his mind he acknowledged that he'd just had the most incredible sex of his life. However, he was aware that the same could not necessarily be said for Lissa.

Had it really been her first time? His brain could not process what had happened. He'd never lost control so spectacularly. The questions in his mind demanded answers. If Lissa had been a virgin, as he suspected, what was her agenda? Women always wanted a piece of him. He'd learned that lesson when he was sixteen. Unwanted memories surfaced. Marina's triumphant smile, and the sickening realisation that she had taken advantage of his tender feelings for her.

He lifted himself off Lissa and rolled on to his back. He had to know the truth. 'It was your first time, wasn't it?'

'Yes.' Her voice was a thread of sound.

A host of unwelcome emotions churned inside Takis. Guilt, confusion and anger, mainly with himself but also with Lissa. 'Why didn't you tell me? If I had realised, I would have been gentler.'

'I did tell you,' she said, still in that small voice that made him think he had ruined something that could have been, *should* have been, beautiful.

He swore silently when he remembered how he

had dismissed her claim of sexual innocence. He'd been convinced that she was playing a manipulative game, and perhaps she was, he thought grimly.

'So, what were you hoping for?' His eyes had become used to the semi-darkness and he saw her puzzled expression. 'Did you expect something in return for your virginity?'

'I had no expectations,' she said quietly. 'To be perfectly honest, I found the whole experience underwhelming.'

Underwhelming! Takis's male pride smarted, but he conceded that Lissa had good reason to feel underwhelmed by his performance.

She got up from the daybed and hurried over to where her dress was a glittering heap next to the pool. Cursing beneath his breath, he pulled his trousers on and strode after her.

'What are you doing?'

She had stepped into her dress and was struggling with the zip. 'Leaving, of course. I can't go back to my room naked. Oh, this wretched zip.'

'Careful, or you will rip the material.'

'Like you care!' She slapped his hand away when he tried to help. The zip was stuck halfway up her dress. She clutched the bodice against her breasts with one hand and picked up her shoes with the other. 'Goodnight.' She swung round and promptly tripped over the hem of her skirt, which was too long without her high heels.

Takis caught her before she fell and turned her to

face him. The glimmer of tears in her eyes tugged sharply on his conscience.

She had been speaking the truth when she had told him she was a virgin.

And she had been speaking the truth when she'd said she wasn't expecting anything from him. His instinctive accusation had been wrong.

Which meant that he had behaved appallingly. He released his breath on a ragged sigh as a single tear slipped down her cheek. 'Don't go,' he said gruffly. 'Stay and talk to me.'

She shook her head, but she did not move away from him, and he felt a faint tremor run through her slender body when he put his hand on her waist. 'What is there to talk about?' she whispered. 'I'm done, Takis.'

But he wasn't done with her. Nowhere near, in fact. 'You could start by explaining why the tabloids printed all those stories about your private life, which were patently not true.'

She avoided his gaze. 'It's complicated.'

'That doesn't surprise me, *koúkla mou,*' he said drily. He had thought he knew everything there was to know about Lissa Buchanan, but she confounded him and intrigued him more than any woman ever had.

He threaded his fingers through hers and led her over to a glass door that opened directly into the master bedroom of the penthouse suite. When he switched on the bedside lamp he was struck by how fragile Lissa looked. Her blue eyes were huge and shimmered with tears. She tucked her hair behind her ear, and something moved inside Takis as his gaze lingered on her delicate features with those exquisite cheekbones.

'I'm sorry your first time was a disappointment.' Takis felt a need to put his arms around her and simply hold her, but he sensed that her composure was close to breaking. He ran his finger lightly down her cheek. Her skin was as soft as a peach and he liked the soft flush that bloomed on her face. He liked it way too much.

His voice deepened. 'I regret my crass behaviour. If I had realised…' He shook his head. 'I listened to gossip and rumour and did not take your inexperience into account.'

CHAPTER SIX

LISSA'S LEGS GAVE way, and she sank down on to the edge of the bed. The stinging sensation between her thighs had eased, but the restless ache there was worse. She felt unfulfilled, overemotional and a little bit sick.

She did not know what she was doing here, why she had stayed with Takis instead of insisting on returning to her room. She did not understand why she had given herself to him and become the kind of woman her grandfather had believed she was. She had always been a disappointment to Pappoús, and now she was disappointed with herself. All the reasons why she had agreed to have casual sex with a man she hardly knew now seemed flimsy, and she felt cheap.

She tried again to pull up her zip, but it wouldn't budge, and she held the bodice of her dress tightly against her breasts. Takis drew up a chair close to the bed and sat down, stretching his long legs out in front of him. When she darted a glance at him, his expression was unreadable, but she sensed that he was angry, although whether with her or himself she couldn't tell.

He folded his arms across his bare chest, drawing her attention to the ripple of muscles beneath his satiny skin. 'You owe me an explanation.'

Lissa flinched at his steely tone. 'I don't owe you anything.'

He said nothing and she let out her breath slowly when it occurred to her that Takis was the only person who had asked her for the truth. Her grandfather had believed every dirty lie printed about her, and even her brother and sister had avoided mentioning her private life whenever juicy details were aired in public.

'It started when I was seventeen,' she said flatly. 'I was invited to a party by a guy called Jason. He was a singer, and I had been to some of his gigs in bars around Oxford. All the girls at school fancied him and I was amazed when he showed an interest in me.'

Anger made tears prick her eyes as she remembered how gullible she had been and how flattered she'd felt when Jason had asked her to be his date at his party.

'He was trying to break into the music business and had his own record label funded by his millionaire father,' she told Takis. 'I was unaware that a photographer from a music magazine and a journalist who worked for a local newspaper had been invited to the party. Jason plied me with alcohol. I thought I would look sophisticated if I drank cocktails, but I got horribly drunk. I don't remember who persuaded me to take my dress off and dance on the table in my underwear.'

She bit her lip. 'Jason suggested we go outside for some fresh air. I let him kiss me, but I'm sure I didn't agree to him taking my bra off. There was a lot of fuss and people and flashing lights, but I was too out of it to know what was happening. Luckily, one of my friends insisted on driving me home.'

Lissa dropped her gaze from Takis's impenetrable stare. 'The next day, the headline on the local newspaper was something along the lines of *Singer's Sex Romp with Star-Struck Groupie* and there was a photo of me, half-naked and in a compromising position with Jason on the bonnet of his father's Rolls-Royce.'

She had felt mortified and *used* when she'd realised that Jason had set her up. 'It was bad enough that I had been humiliated in my home town, but worse was to come. A tabloid newspaper got hold of the photo and they published an interview with Jason in which he said that I was an obsessed fan who had stalked him and begged him for sex because he was famous.'

Takis frowned. 'I assume the guy lied because if he had admitted that nothing happened between you there would not have been a scandalous story and he wouldn't have got exposure in the national press.'

'That's exactly it.' Something loosened in Lissa's

chest, like a knot that had been tightly tied unravelling. 'It was a fantastic publicity stunt for Jason. Radio stations started playing his music and he was even offered a place on a reality TV show.'

'Why didn't you deny the story and demand that the newspapers retract it?'

'I didn't know who to make a complaint to. And, anyway, no one would have believed me. My own grandfather didn't.' She grimaced. 'When Pappoús saw the picture of me in the papers he was furious and accused me of bringing shame on the family. He said my behaviour could damage his reputation, the reputation of the company. Not once did he question if what had been written about me was true. I was still at school, for heaven's sake. But he was so ready to believe the worst of me, so I let him.'

'You should have been able to count on him to defend you,' Takis said in a clipped voice. Lissa wondered if he was talking from experience.

Pappoús's failure to protect her when she had needed his support had been the most hurtful part of the whole unedifying episode. In her mind Lissa heard her grandfather's coldly condemning voice.

You always want to be the centre of attention, just like your father. I never liked him, and I was disappointed when your mother married him. He won a few prizes for showjumping, but he didn't have the work ethic to succeed in business, and you take after him.

Lissa realised that Takis was waiting for her to

continue. 'A result of my unwanted fame was that my photograph was spotted by a scout for a model agency. Their client was a well-known cosmetics company. Sirène were looking for a fresh face to launch their new brand, and they chose me. The brief was a sassy, city girl with an attitude, so I acted the part to convince everyone I was that girl.'

She shrugged. 'I went to parties and met loads of handsome men, but I wasn't interested in any of them. Everyone was playing a game, trying to get noticed and desperate to boost their profile. I was a model for a famous brand and that made guys want to be photographed with me. In the world of celebrity there is no such thing as bad publicity.

'Whenever a scandalous story about me appeared in the tabloids, my grandfather called to say how ashamed he was of me. The *only* times he phoned were to give me a lecture and tell me that I would never amount to anything. I realised that I could get Pappoús's attention by behaving badly. But he had no right to judge me,' she said bitterly. 'He never knew the real me.'

Takis leaned forward in the chair and his grey eyes glittered beneath his thick lashes. 'So who is the real Lissa Buchanan? Why weren't you interested in any of those other men you met at parties?'

'There was no spark,' Lissa admitted. 'I never felt attraction, awareness, whatever you want to call it... until I saw you at my sister's wedding.' She looked away from him. 'But I was wrong.'

He frowned. 'In what way?'

'I thought you felt the spark too. But just now when we...' She felt her face burn. 'It was fairly obvious that I didn't know what to do. The earth didn't move for you...so I must have been mistaken to think you desired me.'

Takis swore. 'The issue was that I desired— *desire*—you too much.' At her puzzled look, he said roughly, 'I have never lost control like that before. The world didn't just move, it spun off its axis. I was impatient, desperate, and they are not words that I have ever used, let alone felt.'

He stood up and raked his hand through his hair. 'Why did you choose *me* as your first lover? Did you get swept up in the romance of the wedding and mistake the sexual attraction between us for love?'

Lissa shook her head. 'I don't believe in love at first sight. How can you fall in love with someone when you know nothing about them? When you know nothing about yourself? I am not the party girl the tabloids made me out to be, but I spent a long time pretending to be that person, and the truth is I don't know who I am,' she admitted.

She met Takis's gaze and said candidly, 'When my grandfather died, I made the decision to take charge of my life and make choices that feel right for me. I chose to have sex with you because I wanted to.' She smiled ruefully. 'And because you are incredibly attractive and sexy, and you promised me one perfect night.'

Takis looked faintly stunned for a few seconds, but then he walked over to the bed and took her hands in his, drawing her to her feet. 'A promise that I have every intention of fulfilling,' he said softly. 'Will you allow me to make love to you with the consideration and care that I should have shown you the first time, Lissa *mou*?'

Her foolish heart skipped a beat to hear him call her *his* Lissa. She wasn't his and never would be. But everything she had told Takis was true. She was on a journey of self-discovery and curious to explore her sensuality. Instead of replying to his question, she lifted herself up on to her toes so that her face was almost level with his and pressed her lips to his mouth.

He immediately took control of the kiss and made a muffled sound in his throat as he slid his tongue between her lips and explored the moist interior of her mouth with mind-blowing eroticism.

Lissa had not entirely believed Takis when he'd told her that he had lost control because he'd wanted her too much. But now the spark blazed into an inferno and his passion scorched her. His mouth and hands were everywhere on her body; his lips moved over her jaw and cheek before sliding up to explore the sweet spot behind her ear, while his fingers gripped the top of her dress and tugged it down to her waist.

He cupped her bare breasts in his big hands and rubbed his thumb pads over her nipples, making them instantly hard. Lissa was desperate for him to replace his fingers with his mouth. She flushed with embarrassment when she realised that she had spoken out loud.

Takis gave a throaty laugh. 'Patience, *koúkla mou*. Good things happen to those who wait.'

'I don't want to wait,' she muttered. 'I want you.'

He muttered something incomprehensible as he stripped off his trousers and tumbled her down on to the bed, removing her dress completely. His body was a symphony of sleek, bronzed skin and impressive musculature, and he was unashamedly aroused. Anticipation sent a quiver through Lissa when he skimmed his hand over her stomach and pushed her thighs apart. He claimed her mouth again in an intensely sensual kiss that drove every thought from her mind, and she gave herself up to the exquisite sensation of Takis gently parting her womanhood and sliding a finger into her slick heat.

His caresses soon had her body clamouring for more, and the ache low in her pelvis became an insistent throb that she instinctively knew only his complete possession would assuage. But when she tried to pull him down on top of her, he laughed softly and shifted his position so that he was kneeling over her. She snatched a breath when he bent his head and kissed his way along her inner thigh, higher and higher until he flicked his tongue over her ultra-sensitive clitoris.

Lissa made a choked sound and gave up trying

to tug his head away from between her legs. She ran her fingers through his luxuriant black hair and arched her hips towards his mouth as he pleasured her in the most intimate way imaginable. Takis reawakened her desire with his wicked tongue, and she curled her fingers into the satin sheet as pleasure built inside her and became an unstoppable, irresistible force. It was too much, not enough, she wanted more, wanted… Bliss.

She came hard against his mouth and gave a sharp cry as her orgasm made her shake from head to toe. But her body sensed there was something more than this sweet delight, something even better.

As if he'd read her mind, Takis lifted his head and murmured, 'That was just a taster, *koúkla mou*. And you taste like nectar.' He donned a condom with a swift efficiency that reminded Lissa he had done this countless times with countless women. She wished that she were more experienced and knew how to pleasure him.

But her insecurity dissolved when she saw the hunger glittering in his eyes. 'Tell me if it hurts and I'll stop,' he murmured as he positioned himself between her thighs, and she felt the swollen tip of him press against her opening. This time there was no sharp sting, just a wonderful feeling of fullness as he eased slowly forward. It felt so unbelievably good. She realised that she had been holding her breath, and when she relaxed and her eyes met his, it was like the final link of the connection between them.

Body and soul, except that Takis had insisted he did not have a soul.

'It doesn't hurt,' she assured him. 'Don't stop.'

He withdrew from her almost completely and then thrust again, a little harder this time, making her gasp as she realised how powerful he was. He filled her, completed her, took her over with each measured stroke as he set a devastating rhythm.

Reality faded, and Lissa decided that if none of this was real, if Takis's big body driving into her was simply an erotic dream, then it did not matter if she arched her hips to take him even deeper inside her and wrapped her legs around his back so that they moved together in perfect synchrony. Each thrust took her closer to a place that hovered frustratingly out of reach. Her breaths came in sharp pants, and she dug her fingers into his shoulders.

Sensations were building to a crescendo deep within her and tiny ripples of pleasure began to ripple out from her central core. Takis slipped his hand between their joined, sweat-slicked bodies and found her hidden pleasure zone. One flick of his thumb and simultaneously another powerful thrust of his body drove her to the edge. He kept her there for seconds that seemed to last for eternity before he gave a final twist of his hand, and she shattered.

The intensity of pleasure was beyond anything Lissa had imagined she could feel. As the shudders of sexual rapture slowly subsided, she realised that Takis had not finished. He started to move again, supporting his weight on his elbows as he set a pace that was wilder than before. Faster. Harder.

Her body welcomed each thrust of his steel length and impossibly she felt her desire stir again. She gloried in his possession and held nothing back. She was his. The words were a litany inside her head, and she whispered them into his mouth when he claimed her lips once more and kissed her deeply. He reared above her, his jaw clenched and his eyes gleaming hotly, and then he gave a savage groan as his big body juddered, and Lissa trembled beneath him as she followed him into the fire.

For a long time afterwards he remained on top of her and their bodies were still joined. His mouth was pressed against her neck and she felt the thunderous beat of his heart gradually slow. Eventually, he moved across the mattress to deal with the condom. His silence stretched Lissa's nerves and she wondered if there was a protocol she should follow. Her inexperience of the situation made her tense and turned Takis into an ominously silent stranger.

'You were right.' Her voice sounded over-bright.

He turned towards her and propped himself up on one elbow. 'About what?'

'You are good at sex.'

'I would take that as a compliment, except I know you have nothing to compare my performance with,' he said with amusement.

She quickly lowered her lashes to hide the emotional storm raging inside her. 'Well, I wasn't disappointed.' She strove for the same cool tone that he had used, as if she could convince herself that she was unaffected by the passion they had shared.

Takis lifted his hand and brushed her long fringe off her face. 'Neither was I disappointed. But I knew I wouldn't be. At Jace and Eleanor's wedding I don't know how I kept my hands off you, and later when I drove you back to the hotel…'

A dark flush ran under his skin. 'I don't usually come on to a woman so strongly. The truth is that I had desired you before we ever met. For a while, your face was on billboards everywhere, department stores, airport lounges, and whenever I turned on a TV it seemed that there was an advert showing the face of Sirène. You. Beautiful, sexy…every woman wanted to be like you and every man wanted you.'

'They wanted who they thought I was. My image was created by a PR agency and accepted without question by the media. Until you, no one ever asked or cared who I really was.'

Takis frowned. 'But then, quite suddenly it seemed, your photograph was replaced with that of another model on adverts for the cosmetics brand, and there were rumours you had been dropped as their repre-sentative.'

Lissa shifted up the bed and leaned against the headboard. She knew it was ridiculous to feel shy after what she and Takis had done but she pulled the sheet over her breasts.

'My contract with Sirène was for three years, but

I became ill a few months before it was due to finish. I lost a lot of weight, and there were other unpleasant symptoms. I felt anxious a lot of the time and my body would tremble uncontrollably. The tabloids jumped to the conclusion that I was a drug addict.'

'Are you fully recovered from your illness?'

'I have an overactive thyroid. It's a lifelong condition, but it is controlled with medication and I have regular check-ups with my GP.'

'Did you hope to return to modelling?' Takis asked.

'I was offered another contract, but my grandfather had died, leaving Eleanor as head of Gilpin Leisure. I jumped at her offer of the position of assistant manager at Francine's hotel.'

Lissa gave him a wry smile. 'You look surprised. I didn't get the job through nepotism. While I was modelling, I also studied hospitality management. Eleanor gave me a trial period, and I have shown that I can run the hotel successfully. My grandfather refused to give me a chance,' she said bitterly. 'But I proved him wrong. When Eleanor married Jace she appointed me as general manager of the hotel.'

She fell silent, feeling embarrassed that she'd probably bored Takis with her life story. He'd admitted that he had desired her when he'd seen photos of her as a beauty model. She had been his fantasy woman…he must have been disappointed when he'd discovered that she was a virgin.

He swung his legs off the bed and did not say

anything as he stood up and walked into the en suite bathroom. Lissa stared at the door, which he'd shut behind him, and wondered if he was giving her a subtle message that it was time for her to leave.

She stood up gingerly and picked up her dress from the floor, to discover that the silk lining was caught in the zip and no amount of tugging would free it. Takis walked back into the bedroom and lifted his brows in silent query when he saw her clutching her dress.

'I don't know what happens next.' She bit her lip. 'I was going to go back to my room.'

'What happens next is that you are going to soak in the bath I have run for you.' His smile made Lissa's heart perform a somersault. The wolf looked almost gentle. 'I thought you might be feeling sore.' He held out his hand to her, and after a brief hesitation she placed her fingers in his and allowed him to lead her into the bathroom.

The bath was a huge, sunken affair, filled to the brim with foaming, fragrant bubbles. 'First we went in the pool, and now I am to have a bath. I'll look like a prune,' Lissa joked to disguise her uncertainty as she stepped into the tub. The mirror revealed that her usually sleek bob was dishevelled, and her mascara was smudged. It was a far cry from when she had been the glamorous face of Sirène.

She looked different and she felt different. It wasn't just the slight tenderness between her legs; she felt as though she had been set free from the rules she'd imposed on herself because she'd needed to prove that she was better than her grandfather's opinion of her. There was a whole great mess awaiting her in the morning, she thought ruefully. But the way Takis was looking at her made her forget everything and focus on him when he joined her in the bath.

'You have never looked more beautiful than you do right now.' He gently touched the red patches on her breasts where his beard had scraped her. 'Your skin is so pale, and I have left my mark on you.'

Not only on her skin, but she did not tell him that she would never forget him. Perhaps every woman remembered their first lover, she thought. But then Takis kissed her and she stopped thinking. He drew her down into the foaming water and picked up a sponge, which he slid over every inch of her skin, paying particular attention to certain areas of her body until she was trembling with longing.

She gasped when he slipped his hand between her thighs and his fingers unerringly found her molten heat. Her own hands were not idle, and she enjoyed making him groan when she touched him, tentatively at first, but she became bolder and circled his thick shaft with her fingers.

'Enough,' he growled. He lifted her on to his lap so that she was straddling his thighs and her pelvis was flush with his. His lips paid homage to her breasts as he entered her with a hard thrust. Water sloshed over the sides of the bath, and the bathroom floor was flooded by the time he scooped her into his arms and carried her through to the bedroom.

Lissa wished the night would last forever. But when the first glimmer of light in the sky heralded the dawn, she studied Takis's autocratic features, which were softer in sleep, and stole one last kiss from his lips before she slid out of bed. He had insisted that he only wanted one night with her, and she could not bear to stay there, only for him to remind her of that. She held her breath when he stirred, but he did not wake up, and she quickly pulled on one of the hotel's bathrobes, gathered up her dress, under-wear and shoes and let herself out of the penthouse.

CHAPTER SEVEN

SUNLIGHT DANCING ACROSS his face woke Takis from a dreamless sleep. Too often his nights were disturbed by nightmares of Giannis trapped by the flames in the burning house. But this morning he felt a deep sense of contentment. The pleasurable ache in his muscles was not surprising after he'd spent hours making love to Lissa. Sex with her had been incredible. But now there were protocols that he hoped she understood.

From experience, Takis knew that waking in the morning with a new lover could be tricky. Women who had seemingly been happy to accept his no-strings rule the night before sometimes turned into clinging vines when it was time to say goodbye. The situation with Lissa was more complicated because she had given her virginity to him.

The possessive feeling that swept through him was inexplicable. The gift of her innocence had been unasked for, and he was appalled that on a deeply fundamental level he liked the fact that he was the first man she'd slept with.

Remembering her passionate response when he'd made love to her made him instantly hard. Lissa may have been a virgin, but she had proved a willing and eager pupil and she'd quickly learned how to please him. He had known from her husky moans and the way she'd trembled in the throes of every orgasm he'd given her that she had enjoyed the night as much as he had.

He rolled on to his side, expecting to find her lying next to him, but there was just a faint indentation on the pillow where her head had been. She was not in the bathroom or outside by the pool and her sequinned dress and shoes were missing, which could only mean one thing.

Takis swore. Once again Lissa had surprised him, and he did not like surprises. Had she left without waking him because she was upset? The idea made him feel uncomfortable, but it had been her decision to sleep with him, he reminded himself. She was not his responsibility, but that did not stop him selecting her number on his phone.

She answered on the fifth ring. Evidently she had not been expecting him to call. 'Takis? Good morning. How are you?'

He gritted his teeth. Anyone listening to her cool voice would think she was talking to a casual acquaintance instead of the man she'd spent the night having passionate sex with.

'I was surprised when I woke and found you had gone.'

'I thought that was the idea,' she said quietly. 'I'm in a taxi on the way to the airport for my flight back to England. You were fast asleep when I left, and I decided not to disturb you.' There was a pause, and then, 'I should probably go. Thank you for a perfect night.'

'It was my pleasure,' he said drily.

Forty minutes later, Takis leaned back in the plush leather seat of the helicopter that was taking him to Athens. He could not understand why he was in such a foul mood. The night he'd spent with Lissa had lived up to all his expectations, and it should have been enough. It *was* enough, he told himself. He had never needed anyone. And no one needed him. He avoided close relationships because if he did not allow himself to care, he couldn't be hurt or feel responsible for someone else's happiness. He was better off alone, and he had never doubted it.

When he walked into his apartment on the top floor of a modern development he owned in the city centre, he acknowledged that the sleekly luxurious but impersonal decor reflected his ethos on life and relationships. He did not form attachments and he shunned all ties. It was true that he'd bought his villa on Santorini because he had been drawn to its picturesque charm. The agent dealing with the sale had remarked that the villa with extensive gardens and access to a private beach would be an ideal family home for when Takis married and had children.

But that wasn't going to happen. He had no need of a wife. Work was the only mistress he cared about. Success was satisfying, but nothing could fill the emptiness inside him. He didn't want it filled. He deserved it.

Lissa was the most complicated, confusing and confounding woman he'd ever met, Takis frequently reminded himself over the following weeks. He was determined to put her out of his mind and focused on his latest project, the acquisition of a hotel and leisure complex in Santorini that he'd had his eye on for a long time. The negotiations over the price he was willing to pay were lengthy and intense, and when the deal was finally signed, he celebrated on the neighbouring island of Mykonos, where some fifteen years ago he had bought his first hotel in the Perseus chain.

Sipping vintage champagne in the hotel's nightclub, Takis acknowledged that he was at the top of his game. He was a self-made multimillionaire, and any of the women in the club would be his with little effort on his part, but none of them captured his interest.

In an effort to forget Lissa, he had dated several beautiful women, and there had been occasions when he'd been snapped by the paparazzi leaving a club with a stunning brunette or a gorgeous redhead. But the tabloids were unaware that he had escorted his dates home at the end of the evening and politely declined all invitations and pleas to stay the night.

He finally admitted to himself that he missed Lissa, which was crazy because he usually never gave an ex-lover a second thought. He had tried keeping his distance from her, but he found himself thinking about her a lot.

Evidently she had taken him at his word when he'd stipulated that he only wanted one night with her, and she hadn't called or messaged him. But that hadn't stopped Takis's heart lurching whenever his phone pinged, and his disappointment when Lissa's name did not appear on the screen inevitably soured his mood.

The situation could not continue, he decided. He would have to see her again, and a new business deal he was on the verge of completing would give him the perfect opportunity to get in touch with her. Overfamiliarity bred boredom, he told himself. If he had an affair with Lissa, he was confident that her novelty would wear off and he would be freed from the unaccountable hold she had on him.

Lissa glanced out of her office window at the rain beating against the glass. The dismal weather reflected her mood, which turned even bleaker when she looked at her computer screen. The photo of Takis with a beautiful woman clinging to his arm was in a Greek newspaper that Lissa was reading online. She did not know why she tortured herself with needing to know what he was doing, and with whom. It was bad enough that every time she spoke to her sister, Eleanor recounted another story about Takis's love life that had appeared in the gossip columns.

Frustrated with her inability to get over him, Lissa deleted the screen image of Takis's starkly handsome face. Since she'd returned to Oxford after spending the night with him at the Pangalos hotel she had focused on work. In an effort to keep busy, she had also enrolled in an interior design course and discovered that she had a natural flair for design.

At school, art had been her passion, and she'd planned to study design at university. But she had got caught up in her modelling career and at the same time had decided to study hotel management because she'd hoped that when she showed her grandfather her qualifications he would be impressed and apologise for doubting her ability to work for the family hotel business. Pappoús had died without knowing how hard she had tried to win his approval, Lissa thought heavily. In many ways she was glad. She had spent too much of her life feeling unwanted by her grandfather, lacking self-worth.

Her phone pinged, and her heart flipped as she wondered if Takis had sent her a message. He hadn't, and she felt angry with herself for hoping that he had. She had wasted enough time moping over him and it had to stop. On impulse she decided that maybe she should accept an invitation to dinner from Andrew, a solicitor she had met at the sports club. She picked up her phone but hesitated before placing it back down on her desk without making the call. Andrew was a nice guy, and it wouldn't be fair to have dinner with him while she was fixated on a devilishly sexy Greek.

Organising the staff rotas was not Lissa's favourite task, but she was glad of the distraction as she opened the relevant computer file. The head chef and sous chef had had an argument and she tried to make sure they were on different shifts, but tonight the hotel was hosting a dinner for a hundred and fifty guests and Ben and Alex would have to work together. Sorting out issues among the staff was a part of hotel management that Lissa knew she did not excel at. It was probably her own insecurity that made her want to please everyone, she thought ruefully.

Her phone rang and she quickly quashed the hope that it was Takis. She smiled when her sister's name flashed on to the screen. 'I have two pieces of news,' Eleanor said after they had exchanged greetings. She sounded excited. 'I'm pregnant.'

'That's wonderful! How does Jace feel about becoming a father?'

'We are both over the moon. I'm expecting a little girl.'

'Oh, El, I'm so pleased for you. Are you suffering much with pregnancy symptoms?'

'Not really. In fact, I didn't realise I was pregnant for a while. But I can't stand the smell of coffee.'

Lissa glanced at the cup of cold coffee on her desk that she had been unable to drink. The effects of an unpleasant stomach bug were still lingering, and she had gone off coffee. 'What is your other news?'

There was a slight hesitation before Eleanor spoke. 'I have decided to sell Francine's. Jace intends to concentrate on running his property development business, and I want to be a full-time mum when the baby comes. But I'll ensure you remain as manager of the hotel.'

'Surely that will be a decision for the new owner.'

'Takis assured me that all the staff will be offered new contracts with his company.'

Lissa's heart clattered against her ribs. 'Takis? Do you mean that *he* is buying Francine's?' She must have misunderstood, she told herself frantically.

'Yes, he is keen to add the Oxford hotel to his Perseus chain.'

'But he can't. You can't sell Francine's…' Lissa tasted blood in her mouth where she had bitten down hard on her lip.

'I'm sorry, I didn't realise you'd be so upset. I know that the hotel is part of Pappoús's legacy, but you and he did not see eye to eye.'

'Francine's is a link to our parents,' Lissa choked.

'We have to let them go,' Eleanor said gently. 'It's time to move on. I expect Takis will contact you soon to discuss the management position.'

Somehow Lissa forced a bright voice as she congratulated Eleanor again on her pregnancy, but at the end of the phone call she felt numb with shock. The prospect of having Takis as her boss was mind-blowing. It would be unbearable to work for him and perhaps see him regularly when he visited the hotel. She would have to resign and look for another job. But she did not only work at the hotel. Francine's was her home, and it would be a huge upheaval to leave.

There was a knock on the door, and her assistant, Pat, walked into the room. 'I saw you had left your coffee to go cold. I've brought you another one.'

'Thank you.' Lissa blenched as the strong aroma of coffee assailed her.

'Are you feeling all right? You haven't seemed yourself lately,' Pat asked with a motherly concern that tugged on Lissa's emotions. 'Maybe you should see a doctor.'

'I have an appointment with my GP this after-noon. I had a blood test to check my thyroid levels and I should find out the result today.'

'You young girls don't eat enough, if you ask me. I hope you'll have time for dinner before the func-tion this evening.' Pat paused on her way out of the door. 'The florist has finished arranging the flowers in the dining room. The tables look lovely. It will be a late night for you, I expect.'

It certainly would, Lissa thought with a sigh. Francine's hotel hosted many functions throughout the year, but the Lord Mayor's dinner and dance was the most prestigious event in the calendar. The invi-tations stated carriages at midnight, but Lissa knew she would be helping to clear up after the party until the early hours.

The rain eased off in the afternoon and she decided to walk to her GP's surgery.

'Unfortunately, the results of your blood test went astray, and I have only just received them,' Dr Williams explained. 'Your thyroid levels are higher than they should be, and I will change the dose of your medication.' She hesitated before continuing. 'There's something else. The blood test also shows a positive result for pregnancy.'

Lissa stared at the doctor, feeling sure that she must have misheard. 'I can't be pregnant,' she croaked. 'I have missed a couple of periods, but I wasn't concerned because it has happened before.'

'Certainly, a thyroid condition can affect a woman's menstrual cycle, resulting in light or irregular periods. But you are definitely pregnant.' The doctor gave Lissa a sympathetic smile. 'I can see that this has come as a surprise. I'd like you to make an appointment with the midwife as soon as possible so that you can be booked for an antenatal scan.'

It couldn't be true, Lissa thought numbly. She couldn't be expecting a baby. Takis's baby. But little things fell into place. Her tiredness and odd reaction to certain smells, especially coffee. The feeling in the pit of her stomach when her sister had revealed her own pregnancy. Her breasts were more tender than usual, and when she had shopped for a new bra she'd found that she had gone up a size.

But she *couldn't* be pregnant. Takis had used a condom each time they'd had sex. She froze when she remembered how he had started to make love to her in the bath. Could it have been then? The how and where were not important, she thought heavily. The fact was that the man who had told her quite clearly he never wanted children was the father of her child.

Lissa walked back to Francine's hotel in a daze, barely able to comprehend that a new life was developing inside her. She had never really thought about having a child because she had been advised that her thyroid condition could make it difficult for her to conceive. This baby was a miracle, but Takis was unlikely to see things that way. He was going to be furious when she told him her news.

She remembered the excitement and pride in her sister's voice when Eleanor had announced her pregnancy and said that Jace was delighted. But Lissa did not have a relationship with her baby's father, and she hadn't spoken to Takis for months. In fact, it was four months since she'd slept with him, she realised when she did a mental calculation. It was astonishing that she had reached that stage in pregnancy without being aware she was carrying Takis's baby. To complicate the situation even more, Takis was the new owner of Francine's. Which made him her boss.

It would not be long before her pregnancy was

noticeable. Even if she did not tell him that the baby was his, he might guess, and she had a fair idea of how he would react. She thought of leaving Oxford and looking for another job and somewhere for her and the baby to live. But Lissa's conscience insisted that Takis had a right to know he was going to be a father.

If he refused to support his child, she would manage. She had some savings from when she'd earned a high income as a model, although she'd lent her brother money so that he could clear his debts. Mark was receiving treatment for his gambling addiction and she could not ask him to repay her while he was trying to get his life back on track.

At least she had her inheritance. Her grandfather's will had prevented Lissa from accessing her trust fund until she was twenty-five, but her sister was the trustee and had made the money available to her. It would help when the baby was born. But Lissa knew she would have to go back to work and all her friends who were working mothers went on about how expensive childcare was.

Somehow she got through the rest of the day and tried not to dwell on her secret while there was so much to do, preparing for the Mayor's dinner-dance. But being pregnant was such a momentous, life-altering event and every time she thought about the future she felt terrified. She popped up to her apartment to change her dress for the evening, and when she studied her body in the mirror she noticed signs of her pregnancy that she'd previously missed. Her breasts were fuller, and her usually flat stomach had a small curve. Emotions that she had held back all day flooded through her. She was scared, but also excited at the thought of having a baby.

When she had been diagnosed with an overactive thyroid, and the endocrinologist had explained that the condition could affect her fertility, she had felt sad that she might never be a mother. It had been something she knew she would have to deal with in the future, if she fell in love with a man and wanted to marry and have a family. But against the odds she was pregnant, and she felt awed and thrilled and still not quite able to believe it.

Just before seven o'clock, guests began to arrive and gathered in the bar for cocktails. Lissa checked the dining room, which looked elegant with the tables dressed in white and gold. Once tonight's event was over she would have time to make plans, but for now she must focus on her job.

The door leading to the kitchen flew open and one of the waitresses ran out. 'Miss Buchanan, Ben and Alex had a fight, and Ben has gone.'

Lissa stared at Kate. 'Gone where?'

'I don't know. He stormed out, saying he wouldn't be coming back. What are we going to do about the dinner?'

What indeed? Lissa tried not to panic. The guests were expecting to sit down to a five-course meal, and she was without a head chef. She hurried into the kitchen and found Alex nursing a fat lip. 'You will have to be head chef tonight,' she told him.

'But—' Alex began to protest.

Lissa turned to the junior chef. 'Jo, you will be sous chef. Everyone else will muck in and help, including me.'

She picked up an apron and was about to put it on when a voice that had haunted her dreams came from the doorway.

'You should not be in the kitchen. Do I need to remind you that your duty as manager of the hotel is to be front of house to greet the guests?'

Lissa spun round, and her heart leapt into her throat as she stared at Takis. It was too soon. He shouldn't be here. Not yet. Not before she'd had time to steel herself.

'I… I wasn't expecting you,' she stammered.

His brows rose but the expression on his hard-boned face was unreadable. 'Evidently not,' he drawled. 'I arrived a little while ago and waited for you in your office. But I find you refereeing a fight between the kitchen staff.'

'I—'

'Are you going to call the staff agencies and request a replacement chef?'

'The recruitment offices will be closed now.'

Takis frowned. 'So what *are* you going to do?'

'I'm sure we can manage,' Lissa assured him, trying to sound more confident than she felt with the torrent of emotions building inside her. 'I'll see if I can get hold of Ben and persuade him to come back to work.'

'Don't bother. I never give second chances.' Takis's hard gaze swept around the room and every one of the staff stood a little straighter. 'My name is Takis Samaras, and I am the new owner of Francine's. Tonight you are all on trial. Do well, and you will keep your jobs. But if you fail to meet my expectations, you're out.'

No one said a word, and everyone suddenly became very busy plating up the first course. Lissa hurried out of the kitchen after Takis. He was talking on his phone and she took the opportunity to study him.

He was wearing black trousers and a matching roll-neck sweater, topped with a black leather jacket, and he was as gorgeous and sexy as she remembered. She fancied that his face was leaner, his sharp cheekbones more pronounced, and the predatory gleam in his eyes made him look even more wolflike.

Her body responded to his rampant masculinity. Her nipples tightened and she felt an ache between her thighs. With a flash of despair she wondered why he still affected her so powerfully. Her hand moved involuntarily to her stomach and she tensed when Takis's eyes roved over her. Would he guess her secret? She was conscious that her black velvet dress was a little tight over her breasts.

He slipped his phone into his jacket. 'I've just

spoken to the manager of the hotel I own in London. They have a chef available who could take the head chef's place, but the journey time to Oxford is an hour and a half, and it would probably be nearer to two hours because of some local flooding where the river has burst its banks.'

Lissa suddenly remembered a gastropub beside the river that had had to close temporarily after the cellar had flooded. 'I have an idea,' she told Takis. She took out her phone and found the number for the White Hart. Five minutes later she had arranged with the pub's manager for the head chef to work at Francine's for the evening.

'Good,' Takis said when she explained that she had found a replacement chef. 'But the argument between the kitchen staff should have been dealt with before now. It was your responsibility to take charge of the situation.'

'Ben has had some personal problems…'

'He should not have brought them into the workplace. Your role as general manager is to ensure the smooth running of the hotel. It is not only the kitchen staff who need to impress me if they want to keep their jobs. I expect one hundred percent commitment from everyone, including you.'

'You're a fine one to talk about commitment,' Lissa burst out angrily.

His gaze narrowed on her flushed face. 'I suggest you set aside your personal feelings while you are at work.'

'That won't be hard. I do not have any personal feelings for you.'

He closed the space between them and stared down at her. Lissa had forgotten how tall he was and felt glad that she was wearing four-inch heels.

'We will continue this discussion later,' Takis said in a low, intense voice that sent a quiver of awareness through her.

'Don't,' she whispered, as much to her foolish pounding heart as to him. Her conscience prodded her to tell him about the baby they had conceived that night in Greece. But she could not bring herself to blurt out her momentous news while they were standing in the busy hotel foyer.

'I must go…and do my job,' she said stiltedly as she stepped away from him and hurried off to the cocktail bar to greet the town's mayor and other local dignitaries.

Much to Lissa's relief, there were no further problems, and the dinner-dance was a great success. The guests began to depart at midnight, but it was another hour before the last car to leave turned out of the hotel's gates. Lissa went into the kitchen to check that the staff had transport home. She phoned for a taxi for one of the young waitresses who had stated her intention to walk through the city centre at night alone.

'It's only a ten-minute walk, Miss Buchanan. Taxi drivers charge the earth after midnight.'

'I'll pay for the taxi, Becky. I want to be sure you

arrive home safely.' Lissa glanced across the kitchen and discovered that Takis was leaning against a counter. He was frowning and she guessed he had overheard her conversation and no doubt disapproved. She would let him know that she had paid the waitress's taxi fare personally, and not out of hotel expenses.

By the time she had locked the front door after everyone had gone, Lissa felt sick with tiredness, and her heart sank when she walked past her office and saw Takis sitting behind her desk. His desk now, she silently amended as she stepped into the room.

'These are very good,' he murmured, flicking through her folder of interior design ideas.

'You have no right to look through my private folder,' she said stiffly.

'I do if you were working on your designs when you should have been carrying out your job as the hotel's manager.'

'Those particular sketches are my ideas for refurbishing some of the hotel's bedrooms.' Lissa bit her lip. 'I heard you tell the staff at the end of the shift that their jobs are secure. But what about me? Will I continue to manage Francine's?'

He drummed his fingers against the desk. 'I plan to install an experienced manager from one of my other hotels. Francine's is dated in the way it operates, and frankly it fails to provide the high quality of service that I demand.'

Shocked and dismayed, Lissa closed her eyes,

desperate to stop the tears that threatened to spill from them. She couldn't lose her job. Not now. When she opened her eyes again Takis had moved and was standing in front of her. 'I proved tonight when I found a replacement chef that I can think on my feet. I'm good at my job. You can't fire me,' she pleaded.

He lifted his hand and tucked her hair behind her ear. 'I have other plans for you, *koúkla mou*.'

The spicy scent of his aftershave assailed her senses, and a tremor ran through her when he slid his hand beneath her chin and tilted her face up to his. Lissa's body responded wildly to the sensual promise glittering in his grey eyes as he lowered his mouth towards hers.

With a low cry she pulled away from him. 'No. You don't understand. I need my job at Francine's because I… I'm pregnant.'

Takis rocked back on his heels but he said nothing. His muted reaction was worse than if he'd exploded in rage. Lissa wished he would say *something*. Anything would be better than his ominous silence.

'Congratulations,' he drawled at last. 'Is the father of your child pleased?'

His voice dripped ice, and a shiver ran through Lissa. Did he really not understand what she was telling him?

Shakily she tried again. 'You are the father. I'm having your baby, Takis.' His furious expression shredded her nerves, but she continued. This time with conviction. 'I realise that you probably don't welcome the news. But I intend to support the child on my own. That's why I'm asking you to allow me to keep my job.'

CHAPTER EIGHT

THERE WAS A roaring noise in Takis's ears. He could not think or breathe. He felt the hard thud of his pulse, of his temper rushing like boiling lava through his veins. It could not be true. Lissa must be playing a cruel trick. Hadn't he learned years ago that all women were manipulative? And had once believed Lissa to be the same?

He realised that she was waiting for him to say something. But he could not bring himself to speak. Did not dare. His throat had closed up and his heart was trying to claw its way out of his chest. He stared at her, searching for some sign on her slim figure that she was expecting a child.

There was something different about her, he realised. Earlier tonight when he had seen her again for the first time, he had been stunned by her radiant beauty. The way she had seemed to glow from within.

Theé mou!

Even if she *was* pregnant, there was no way it

was his baby, he reassured himself. He held on to that. His vocal cords relaxed, and he bit out one word. 'No.'

'For God's sake, Takis. There are employment laws in England. Pregnant women have rights, and you can't simply dismiss me.'

'No,' he repeated harshly, trying to convince himself as much as her. 'I am not the father of your baby.'

Lissa seemed to grow taller and she lifted her chin and met his gaze proudly. 'You know damn well that I was a virgin until I met you.'

He could not deny that indisputable fact. But he wasn't fooled by her look of wide-eyed innocence. He couldn't be. 'You must have taken another lover after you slept with me,' he said coldly. The sensation of an iron band crushing his chest was lessening as his brain kicked into gear.

'Do you really believe I hopped into another man's bed immediately after I'd had my first sexual experience with you?' Lissa demanded.

Takis wanted to believe it. The alternative was unthinkable.

'You are the only man I've ever had sex with, and whether you like it or not I am expecting your baby.' She took a step towards him. 'Please believe that I never meant for this to happen. I only found out today and I am as shocked as you.' She placed her hand on her stomach and said softly, 'An accidental pregnancy is not such a terrible thing. We are going to have a baby.'

Rejection roared through Takis. And fear. Gut-wrenching fear. He could not be responsible for a child. Not again.

'I do not want a child. I told you that fatherhood holds no appeal for me.'

He did not doubt that she was pregnant. And now that the initial shock was subsiding, he realised that he did not doubt quite so strongly that the baby was his. Even as he fought against the very idea. He was the most untrusting man on the planet, and yet he had no reason not to trust Lissa. He did trust her. She had never lied to him. But how could *he* be a father after he had behaved so irresponsibly in the past? Takis was certain that he did not deserve to have a child. A child did not deserve him.

'Fine.' Lissa spun round and marched across the office. She had almost reached the door before he realised that she actually intended to walk out.

'Where are you going?'

'To bed.' She put her hand on the door handle and sent him a withering glance over her shoulder. 'I started work at six a.m. yesterday and it is now a quarter to two in the morning, which means that I have been on duty for nearly twenty hours. Does that show enough commitment to my job?' Her sarcastic tone made Takis grit his teeth.

'We have things to discuss,' he bit out.

'What things?' She opened the door. 'I have informed you that I'm pregnant and you stated that you do not want to be a father. So don't be.'

Cursing beneath his breath, he strode after her and slammed the door shut before she could walk out. 'What do you mean? Am I *not* the father? Do not play games with me, Lissa,' he warned her darkly.

She turned to face him. 'This baby might be unplanned, but he will be loved, is already loved by me. I told you about my pregnancy because it was the right thing to do, but I don't want anything from you. I'll go away somewhere, and you will never hear from me again. When my child is older and asks about his father, I will say that you are dead. Better that than for him to find out that he was not wanted by his father.'

Did she mean it? Takis's jaw clenched. Just because Lissa had not made demands yet, it did not mean that she wouldn't do so. He hadn't wanted a child, but a child had been conceived. *His* child. Could he really walk away from his own flesh and blood? The answer hit him like a punch in his solar plexus. Of course he couldn't.

Takis felt the same sense of being caught in a trap that he'd felt when his stepmother had played a cruel game with his teenage emotions. One he had tried to escape by leaving home, leaving the half-brother he'd adored behind. He could never forget or forgive himself for abandoning Giannis to such a terrible fate. Had never confessed what his actions had led to.

He raked his fingers through his hair, unsurprised

that his hand was unsteady. 'Why did you refer to the baby as him?' he asked Lissa.

She shrugged. 'I just have a feeling that it's a boy. I'll be able to find out the baby's sex when I have a scan and I can text you the result if you would like to know.'

She was so cool, Takis thought savagely, aware that his own emotions were dangerously close to exploding. He placed his palms flat against the door on either side of her head and watched her eyes widen in response to the sexual chemistry that had always been a potent force between them, and still was, he acknowledged.

Lissa stared at him. 'If you give me twenty-four hours to pack up my things and write me a reference so that I will be able to get another job, I promise you will never see or hear from me again.'

He believed her. She'd left without waking him after she had given her virginity to him. Lissa was perfectly capable of disappearing, and he would spend the rest of his life wondering if his child was safe or needed his protection. It would be a new kind of hell, a different version of his nightmares.

She sagged against the door and closed her eyes. Takis was struck by how fragile she looked. The dark smudges beneath her eyes were a stark contrast to her pale skin. 'I'm exhausted,' she whispered. 'We both need to calm down. Perhaps we will be able to talk more rationally tomorrow.'

Concern replaced his anger. Lissa was pregnant

LOYAL READER
FREE BOOKS VOUCHER

and Takis acknowledged that his behaviour was unacceptable. Without saying another word, he scooped her off her feet and held her against his chest.

Her lashes flew open. 'What do you think you're doing?'

'You were about to collapse,' he said gently as he opened the door and carried her through the hotel foyer.

Her blue eyes flashed with anger. 'I don't need your help.'

'Yes, you do.' His jaw clenched, determined. Lissa and the baby were his responsibility. *God help them*, he thought grimly. 'You will have to direct me to your living quarters.'

She sighed as if she realised that it was pointless to argue with him. 'Go through the door marked *Private* and there is a lift up to the apartment on the top floor.'

Her head dropped on to his shoulder and she was asleep by the time Takis carried her into the apartment and located her bedroom. He looked down at the silky blonde hair that curled against her delicate jawline. She was so beautiful. He felt a fierce tug of desire in his groin and was furious at his unbidden response to her. This was not the time.

He resented the hold Lissa had over him. He'd come to Oxford intent on rekindling their passion so that he could get her out of his system. But she had dropped the bombshell of her pregnancy and he had no idea how to proceed.

He laid her on the bed and unzipped her dress. She hardly stirred when he removed the dress and her shoes but left her bra and knickers in place. When he pulled the duvet over her, he thought how young she looked. He swore softly. What a god-damned mess.

Takis knew he should try to sleep, but his thoughts were too chaotic. He explored the apartment and in the kitchen found a bottle of brandy, which he carried into the sitting room. Getting blind drunk was tempting but would not solve anything. Lissa was pregnant with his baby. It was his worst nightmare come true.

He remembered the first time he had met his baby half-brother. He had loved Giannis from the moment he'd looked inside the pram and seen a tiny infant with huge, dark eyes. Giannis had grown into a sweet-natured little boy who had adored his big brother.

Takis took a long swig of brandy, unable to hold back the memories that surged into his mind. He had not discovered what had happened until a few days after he'd left his home and travelled to Thessaloniki, where he'd happened to meet someone from the village.

'Will you go back for the funerals?' the man had asked him. 'You haven't heard? There was a fire. Your father tried to escape from the burning house, but he was killed when a wall collapsed on top of him.'

Takis had not cared about the fate of his father.

'You said funerals.' Sick dread had curdled in the pit
of his stomach. *'Did my stepmother...? And Giannis?
Not him, please, no, not him.'* A howl of agony had
been ripped from his throat when the villager shook
his head.

*'Marina and her little son both died in the flames.
It's lucky you were not there, or you could have lost
your life too.'*

Guilt was his punishment, Takis brooded now as
he refilled his glass. He should have stayed at home
to protect Giannis, but in a fit of pique and fury with
his stepmother he'd run away. Oh, he'd told himself
that he was leaving because he wanted a better life
than that of a goat herder, but the truth was that he'd
wanted to pay Marina back for breaking his heart.

When he had returned to the village he had been
overwhelmed with grief at the sight of the blackened
shell of the house, and at the mortuary three coffins.
He'd walked straight past the largest coffin, hesitated
next to the wooden box that held Marina's body and
crumpled to his knees beside the smallest coffin.

It had been so pathetically small. That's what had
struck him the hardest. Giannis had been just five
years old. Imagining his little brother's terror when
he'd woken in the night and found he was trapped by
the flames had fuelled Takis's nightmares ever since.

He prowled around the room and stopped in front
of the bureau where several framed photographs
were displayed. The little girl with pale blonde hair
was unmistakably Lissa, and he guessed that the

attractive couple on either side of her were her parents. They looked a happy family, but family was something Takis had no concept of. He had grown up with a violent father and a stepmother who had tried to seduce him.

How did his upbringing equip him to be a successful parent? The truth was that it did not, which was why he had decided that he would not have children. But he remembered the words Lissa had thrown at him: he was going to be a father, whether he liked it or not.

Perhaps Lissa's pregnancy was a chance for him to atone for his past mistakes, Takis brooded. If he was honest, the responsibility of becoming a father terrified him. But he would not abandon his child like he had abandoned his brother. He must claim his baby.

Fragments of a dream flitted through Lissa's mind. Takis arriving unexpectedly at the hotel, his furious reaction when she'd told him about the baby. Her eyes flew open and she could feel her heart pounding. It hadn't been a dream. Light was filtering through the curtains into her bedroom. She checked the time and was horrified to see that it was ten o'clock before she remembered that the deputy manager would be on duty.

She had been dead on her feet at the end of the dinner-dance. Takis had brought her to the apartment, and he must have removed her dress and put her to bed. Her stomach rumbled, and she knew she should eat for the baby's sake. She wondered if Takis had spent the night in the hotel or whether he had driven back to London. He'd made it clear that he did not want the baby, and there really was nothing for them to talk about. She certainly did not want a maintenance payment from him. She and her baby would be fine on their own, Lissa told herself.

She pulled on her dressing gown and headed for the kitchen but stopped dead when she looked into the sitting room and saw Takis sprawled on the sofa, where he had obviously slept. His shirt was creased and the dark stubble on his jaw was thicker, but his rumpled appearance did not detract from his dangerous sex appeal. Lissa felt her nipples harden, and even though her dressing gown was made of thick towelling she folded her arms over her chest as Takis raked his gaze over her.

'Why didn't you use a room in the hotel?' she asked him. 'Two of the suites were empty.'

'I stayed in your apartment to be close to you in case you needed anything during the night. There was also the possibility that you might try to disappear,' he said drily.

Her legs felt wobbly and she sank down on to the sofa. 'I don't have anywhere to go.' The reality of her situation was sinking in. She would soon be without a job or a home. She supposed she could go and stay with her sister in Greece while she tried to organise her life, but the future was frighteningly uncertain.

Takis shifted along the sofa towards her. 'You are still very pale.' He picked up her wrist. 'Your pulse is going crazy. Is a fast heartbeat normal in pregnancy?'

'I'm not sure.' She did not tell him that his close proximity as he rubbed his thumb lightly over her wrist might be why her pulse was racing. 'My thyroid condition can cause problems during pregnancy and I'll have to have extra check-ups to make sure the baby is developing okay.'

He stood up and grimaced when he ran his hand over his rough jaw. 'I need a shower and a change of clothes, and then we will talk.'

Lissa noticed his holdall, which he must have brought from his car last night. She directed him to the guest bathroom and went to the kitchen to make tea and toast. She reminded herself that they were adults, and without the heightened emotions of the previous night it was surely not beyond them to have a cordial discussion. She would not prevent Takis from seeing his child if he wanted to.

As she carried the tray into the sitting room, it occurred to her that she did not even know if he drank tea. They had created a new life together, but her baby's father was a stranger.

Takis walked into the room, and Lissa's heart crashed against her ribs as she made a mental inventory of him. Faded jeans hugged his lean hips and he wore a grey cashmere sweater that clung lovingly to his muscular chest. His hair was damp from the shower. He had trimmed the stubble on his jaw, but he still looked like a pirate. He was devastatingly attractive, Lissa thought with a rueful sigh that he could still affect her so strongly.

'This is fine, thank you,' he said when she offered to make him coffee if he preferred it to tea. She'd noticed he winced when she explained that she only had instant coffee.

Lissa forced herself to eat half a piece of toast, but it tasted like cardboard and swallowing became an ordeal as her tension grew. 'You wanted to talk,' she reminded him.

He put down his cup, the tea untouched, she noticed.

'You and the baby are my responsibility.'

His coolness quashed her tiny hope that there could be a happy outcome to their conversation. She remembered when he'd made love to her and his eyes had blazed with heated passion. Now Takis was a remote stranger, and Lissa's heart sank when she realised that he viewed her pregnancy as a problem that he was determined to solve.

'I don't want to be your responsibility,' she said sharply. 'I've had enough of feeling like a burden. That's what I was to my grandfather. You don't have to be involved. I have money of my own and, as I told you, I plan to go back to work after the baby is born.'

'How do you propose to combine bringing up a child with a career?'

'I haven't worked out the details yet. But I will

be fine,' Lissa insisted. 'I won't deny you visiting rights if that's what you want.'

He shook his head. 'I have a duty to ensure the welfare of the child we have created and your welfare. There is an obvious solution to the situation we find ourselves in.'

She gave a helpless shrug. 'It's not obvious to me.'

'We will marry as soon as it can be arranged,' Takis said smoothly.

'Marry?' Lissa stared at him incredulously. 'I'm not going to marry you. There's no need.'

His hard-boned face showed no emotion. 'You do not think it is important for the baby to be legitimate?'

'Nobody cares about that these days. Marrying simply to conform to outdated values is a terrible idea.' Without giving him a chance to speak, she said fiercely, 'I don't want to marry you. It's a crazy idea.'

'Nevertheless, it *will* happen.' He sounded implacable, and Lissa felt a ripple of unease. Takis could not make her marry him, she reminded herself. 'Marriage will give us equal parental rights,' he continued. 'If you refuse, I will seek custody of my child.'

She jumped up from the sofa, breathing hard. 'You wouldn't win. Courts rarely separate a baby from its mother unless there are exceptional circumstances.'

'Would you be prepared to risk a legal battle that could drag on for months or even years? The costs involved with solicitors' fees and so on are likely to be exorbitant.'

'I don't believe this,' Lissa said shakily. 'You told me that fatherhood does not appeal to you.'

His jaw clenched. 'It's true I would not have chosen to have a child. But neither of us have a choice. You are pregnant and we must both do what is best for the baby.'

Takis was like a tornado tearing through her life, Lissa thought frantically. She felt agitated and panicky and her heart was beating alarmingly fast. 'I can't breathe,' she gasped. The room was spinning. She flung out a hand to grab hold of the back of the chair.

'Lissa!'

Takis's voice came from a long way off. It was the last thing she heard before blackness engulfed her.

CHAPTER NINE

'ARE YOU SURE the baby is all right?' Lissa asked the nurse who was pushing her in a wheelchair along the hospital corridor.

'Baby is fine. Your pregnancy was constantly monitored while you were in intensive care, but you will feel more reassured when you have an ultrasound scan later today. We'll get you settled in your room first.'

Lissa glanced around the pretty room they had entered. It was decorated in shades of pink and reminded her of a luxury hotel room. 'This doesn't look like a hospital ward.'

'Mr Samaras arranged for you to have a private room,' the nurse explained as she helped Lissa on to the bed. 'Would you like me to put your photographs on the bedside cabinet? Mr Samaras brought them in,' she said as Lissa looked puzzled when she saw two framed photos of her family that had been on the bureau in her apartment at Francine's hotel.

She remembered that whenever she had opened

her eyes Takis had been sitting next to her hospital bed. But her memory was vague. The doctor had explained that she'd been rushed to the hospital by ambulance and admitted to the intensive care unit after she had collapsed.

'You experienced a thyroid storm, which is a rare complication of hyperthyroidism. Your thyroid levels were dangerously high, which caused your blood pressure to soar. The condition can be fatal if it is not treated quickly.' The doctor was confident that Lissa's pregnancy should continue normally with her thyroid condition controlled with medication. Although there was a risk that that she could go into labour prematurely.

'How long have I been in hospital?' she asked the nurse.

'A week. You were very poorly for a few days. That handsome fiancé of yours has been very worried about you.'

Fiancé? Lissa's memory was becoming clearer. Takis had demanded that she marry him, but she had never agreed she would. Thankfully, her baby was unharmed by what had happened to her. She wondered if Takis had been worried about the baby, or if he'd hoped that her illness would put an end to her pregnancy. Tears filled her eyes as she lay back on the pillows.

She must have slept because when she awoke, Takis was sitting on a chair beside the bed. Her heart flipped as she studied him. He was as gorgeous as ever, but there were grooves on either side of his mouth that had not been there a week ago.

'How are you feeling?' he asked. Nothing in his voice or shuttered expression gave a clue to his thoughts.

'Better,' Lissa told him. 'You don't need to be here. I'm sure you must want to go back to Greece to run your business.' She bit her lip when his heavy brows drew together.

'I have stated that you and the child you are carrying are my responsibility.' He ran a hand through his hair. '*Theos!* It is my fault that you nearly died,' he said harshly. Lissa had never seen him so unrestrained.

'How do you work that out?'

'Your thyroid condition means that pregnancy is a higher risk for you. I should have been more careful when we had sex.' A dark flush ran along his sharp cheekbones. 'There was one time in the bath when I was reckless.'

'There were two of us,' Lissa said quietly. 'I was reckless too.' Takis could not spell it out any clearer that he regretted her pregnancy.

The tense silence was broken by a knock on the door, and a nurse entered the room. 'I've come to take you for your ultrasound scan, Miss Buchanan. Would you like your fiancé to accompany you?'

Lissa glanced at Takis. 'Well, do you want to see your baby?'

His eyes narrowed at her challenging tone. He

seemed to be waging an internal battle with himself. 'I would like to be at the scan,' he said in a tense voice.

In the scanning room Lissa had the sense that everything was surreal. She hadn't had much time to assimilate the news that she was pregnant before she'd been taken ill, and the time she'd spent in intensive care was a blur. A nurse helped her on to a bed and the sonographer smeared gel on to her stomach. When she was lying down her bump was barely discernible.

'Every pregnant woman carries differently,' the sonographer assured her. 'But your baby is definitely in there. This is the heart.' She pointed to a tiny, flickering speck on the screen. 'And here we have the head and spine.'

Lissa held her breath. Her eyes were fixed on the image on the screen. It was real. In a few months she was going to have a baby. A little person of her own who she would love, and who would love her. She felt overwhelmed with emotion and fiercely protective of the new life that she would soon bring into the world. A new life she would never let feel like a burden to her.

'The baby is a bit smaller than I would have expected for your dates, but there is no cause for concern at the moment,' the sonographer explained. 'I can tell you the sex if you would like to know.'

Lissa looked at Takis. He had not spoken during the scan and she had no idea what he was thinking.

'It is your decision,' he said. There was nothing in his voice to give a clue to how he felt at seeing his unborn child. Perhaps if they knew whether she was expecting a boy or girl, Takis would feel more of a connection to the baby.

'We would like to know,' Lissa said to the sonographer.

'You are expecting a boy. Congratulations.'

Lissa's heart leapt. A little boy! She wondered what he would be like and imagined a baby with dark hair like his father. She had felt him stiffen when they had been told the baby's gender. How did Takis feel about having a son? She glanced at him and was startled by an expression of stark pain on his face. She turned her head back towards the screen and the image of their tiny son. When she looked at Takis again, his hard features were once more unreadable. But Lissa could not forget his devastated expression or help but wonder what it had meant. Whether he truly feared fatherhood or if it was something more.

He pushed her wheelchair back to her room and ignored her protest that she did not need his help as he lifted her on to the bed. The brief moments when he held her in his arms evoked a sharp tug of longing in Lissa, and she swept her eyelashes down to hide her expression from his speculative gaze.

'Thank you for bringing these from home,' she said, picking up the photographs of her family.

'I thought you might like to have them. How old were you when the photos were taken?'

'Ten. The picture of me with my mum and dad was taken at a gymnastics competition. I'd won a medal and they were so proud of me. Mum had been a gymnastics champion and she encouraged me to take up the sport.'

She held up the other photo. 'This was taken on a family holiday to Ireland before my parents flew to Sri Lanka to celebrate their wedding anniversary. It was the last picture of them before they died.' Her heart gave a pang as she looked at her parents smiling faces.

'You had a close relationship with them?'

'I was the spoiled, youngest child, and my brother and sister probably resented all the attention my parents gave me,' she said ruefully. 'But we were a happy family.' She remembered family events, birthdays and Christmases that her parents had made so magical. They had made her feel safe and secure and loved, and that was what she wanted for her baby.

She looked at Takis. 'Why did you ask me to marry you?'

He frowned. 'You know why. You are pregnant with my baby.'

'Yes, but why insist on marriage—really? I've told you that you don't have to stick around.'

His jaw clenched. 'I will not abandon my child. He is my heir. It would make no difference if you were expecting a girl,' he said before Lissa could speak. 'I am determined to protect my son and provide for him. My business interests have made me wealthy and I can give him a good lifestyle and the best education. Everything that I did not have,' he added.

Lissa nodded. 'I'm not so naive as to think that money and the privileges it brings are not important. But it is far more important that our son grows up knowing that he is loved unconditionally.'

Takis did not respond, but perhaps men did not feel the surge of devotion that expectant mothers felt to their unborn children—that she certainly felt—Lissa mused. It would be different when the baby was born and Takis held his son in his arms. She had to believe that. She wanted to believe they would create a family unit that she had craved after her parents had been cruelly snatched from her.

'I will marry you,' she told him, trying to ignore the lurch her heart gave, the feeling that she had taken a leap into the unknown. 'My brush with death, or at least serious illness, has made me see things more clearly. No one can predict what will happen in life. My parents went on holiday and did not return.'

She swallowed the lump in her throat. 'If we are married and something should happen to me, I'll have the reassurance of knowing that my son will still have his father, and there will be no question over who should bring him up.'

Takis frowned. 'Nothing is going to happen to you.'

'You can't be certain. I'm not being pessimistic, just realistic.' She sighed. 'After my parents died my father's cousin and his wife offered to have me and my brother and sister. But my grandfather was the next of kin and we were sent to live with him. Pappoús didn't want Mark and me, and he only took an interest in Eleanor because he groomed her to take over the family's hotel business.'

Lissa wished Takis would say something. His lack of enthusiasm was a reminder that he believed it was his duty to marry her. She was once again someone's responsibility. At least that's clearly the way he felt. It was a far cry from the romantic dreams she'd had when she'd been a little girl of meeting her Prince Charming. But she'd stopped believing in fairy tales as well as Father Christmas and the Tooth Fairy when her parents had died. More than anything she wanted security for her son. Which meant she must marry her baby's enigmatic father.

'I will make the arrangements for the wedding to take place in Greece,' Takis told Lissa. His voice was clipped, his emotions tightly controlled. He knew from the slight quiver of her bottom lip that she was hurt by his brusqueness.

Frustration surged through him. He had never wanted to marry or have a child, but fate, or more truthfully, his spectacular lack of control when he'd had sex with Lissa and his hunger for her had run wild, meant that he would soon be a husband and a father.

He was going to have a son. The shock of it ripped through him. If he had not attended Lissa's scan, he might have been able to distance his emotions from the situation. But she had looked at him with such fierce hope in her eyes that he'd found himself agreeing to go to the scanning room. And in truth he had been curious to see his child.

It had been worse and at the same time more incredible than he could have imagined. The images on the screen of his baby had been surprisingly clear, and the sight of a tiny beating heart had made his own heart clench. Right then, he had made a silent vow that he would give his life to protect his child, as he should have protected his brother years ago.

Memories slid from their lair in his mind. They were always there, waiting for him to drop his guard, and as soon as he did, they tormented him.

'Where are you going? It's night-time.'

Giannis's sleepy voice had come from the mattress on the floor that he'd shared with Takis.

'Can I come with you?'

'Not this time, agoraki mou.' Takis had knelt and pulled his little brother into his arms. 'I have to go away for a while. Don't cry. I promise I will come back for you soon.'

He'd felt Giannis's hot tears on his neck as sobs

had shaken the boy's skinny body. 'I don't want you to go, Takis. Stay with me...'

That was the last time Takis had held his brother. He had returned to the village only once, to carry Giannis's coffin into the church. Even after all this time his grief was still raw. He had betrayed an innocent child's faith, his word had meant nothing and the memory of Giannis's tears would haunt him forever.

Lissa was looking at him and he did not understand why he felt such an urge to confide his secret shame to her. There could be no absolution for what he had done. He glanced at the photograph of her with her parents. There had been so much love in her voice when she'd spoken about them.

Something inside him cracked as he thought of the reason why she had agreed to marry him. Marriage would ensure that he was the baby's legal guardian. Lissa had suffered the devastating loss of her parents, and she was determined to spare her child from rejection, which was how her grandfather had treated her.

'I give you my word that I will protect our son, always,' he said gruffly. He would make sure he kept it this time.

Her blue eyes widened. Those beautiful blue eyes, the colour of the summer sky, that had cast a spell on him the instant he'd met her. But he would not allow her to bewitch him with her mix of innocence and sensuality again, Takis assured himself. He could not.

'And love.' She stared at him, and he wondered if she had noticed him flinch at the word. 'You will love our son, I hope. That's the deal.'

It was not his deal and never would be, but Takis did not tell her that his heart was buried on a mountainside with a little boy he had betrayed.

'You should rest,' he said briskly, avoiding Lissa's gaze. 'As soon as you are well enough to be discharged from hospital we will fly to Athens so that I can organise the necessary paperwork for us to marry. I would prefer a simple ceremony and a minimum of fuss.'

'I'd like my sister to be my bridesmaid.' A pink stain ran along her cheekbones, emphasising her delicate beauty. 'Our marriage is a practical solution to the situation we find ourselves in. But Eleanor won't understand. She married Jace for love. I don't want her to worry about me, especially while she is pregnant. It would be better if we pretend that our marriage is real.'

'There is no reason why anyone else should know the truth of our relationship,' Takis agreed. But as he roamed his eyes over Lissa another truth hit him. A strap of her nightgown had slipped down to reveal a slim shoulder and the smooth slope of her breast, and he felt a white-hot flash of desire in his groin.

This was the reason he found himself in a situation that required him to marry, even though he had never wanted a wife, and still did not, Takis thought furiously. This uncontrollable desire that he'd never felt so intensely for any other woman. When he had met Lissa months ago he'd been unable to resist her sensual allure, but he'd limited himself to one night with her. However, their one perfect night had resulted in her conceiving his child and had changed the course of his life.

But he *would* control his body's response to her that made his heart rate quicken and his blood thunder through his veins. He was determined that their marriage would be on his terms, but Lissa's suggestion to allow other people to believe they were marrying for conventional reasons made sense, Takis decided.

'We will live in Greece,' he told her. 'I own a penthouse apartment in Athens, but it is not a suitable place to bring up a child. Do you have any preferences on the kind of house you would like?'

'So I am to have a choice?'

He narrowed his eyes to hide his irritation at her sarcastic tone. 'I would like to bring up my son in Greece. I assumed you understood that, but if you object strongly I suppose I can consider moving my business base to England.'

'I don't mind living in Greece. But I want us to discuss things. I am an adult, not a child who you can tell what to do,' Lissa said with some asperity. 'Marriage is about compromise.'

'I will try to remember,' he said evenly. Compromise was not a word in Takis's vocabulary, but he would put his ring on Lissa's finger and thereby claim his child before she discovered that fact.

CHAPTER TEN

THE WEDDING TOOK place at the civic hall in Athens a month after Lissa had been discharged from hospital and Takis had brought her to Greece. Jace and Eleanor flew in from their home in Thessaloniki, and Lissa shed emotional tears when she hugged her sister.

'It's so exciting that our babies will be born only a few months apart,' Eleanor said when they were in the waiting room before the ceremony. She gave Lissa a thoughtful look. 'I'll admit I was surprised when you told me you are pregnant. I didn't realise that you and Takis were together, although it was obvious at the charity ball that the two of you couldn't take your eyes off each other. Was it love at first sight?'

'It was,' Takis answered for Lissa. She tensed as she looked around and found he was standing behind her and must have overheard the conversation with her sister. He smiled urbanely at Eleanor. 'At your wedding to Jace when I was the best man and

Lissa the chief bridesmaid, we both felt an instant connection, didn't we, *agapi mou*?'

He met Lissa's startled gaze and the indefinable expression in his eyes made her tighten her fingers on the bouquet of freesias that he had surprised her with before they'd driven to their wedding. She reminded herself that they were pretending to be in love so as not to arouse her sister's suspicions. Lissa knew that Eleanor would be concerned if she guessed the real reason for her decision to marry Takis.

They both wanted security for their son, but Lissa was starting to realise that she hoped for more than a sterile marriage of convenience. Her pulse accelerated when Takis slipped his arm around her waist. There had been no physical contact between them in the run-up to the wedding when they had lived at the house that Takis had leased in a leafy suburb of Athens.

The rental house was sleek and modern, but in Lissa's opinion the decor was unimaginative. Since she had left her job as manager of Francine's hotel she'd focused on the interior design course she was studying online. There was minimalist and there was boring, she'd told Takis when she ordered brightly coloured cushions to bring life to the living room. Takis had merely raised his eyebrows and disappeared into his study, where he spent most of his time when he was not at the Perseus hotel chain's head office.

Lissa had the sinking feeling that he wanted to avoid her, but she had reminded herself that the situation was odd for both of them. They were almost strangers, but once they were married she hoped they would begin to build a life together and create a family unit ready for when they welcomed their son into the world.

She looked down at the engagement ring on her finger. The previous day her hopes of building a relationship with Takis had been boosted when he'd unexpectedly joined her for dinner. Most evenings she dined alone because he did not return from work until late. But when she had walked into the dining room, she'd found him waiting for her and her heart had performed a somersault.

She had been reminded of the first time she'd met him at her sister's wedding when she had been desperately aware of his smouldering sensuality. Nothing had changed, she'd thought as her pulse had quickened when she'd smelled the distinctive spicy scent of his aftershave.

'I have something for you,' Takis had said after the butler had served the first course and left the room. He'd handed her a small box, and Lissa's heart had thumped when she'd opened it to reveal a ring with a deep blue sapphire surrounded by diamonds.

'It's beautiful,' she'd said huskily.

He'd given her a brisk smile and picked up his wine glass. 'Your sister would think it odd if you did not wear an engagement ring.'

I don't care what anyone else thinks, she had wanted to tell him. For goodness' sake, walk around the table and kiss me! But she hadn't dared say the words out loud. Instead she had slipped the ring on to her finger and sternly reminded herself that their marriage was a practical arrangement and Takis was not likely to have gone down on one knee when he'd presented her with the ring.

Lissa pulled her mind back to the present and realised that Eleanor was speaking to Takis.

'How did you persuade my sister to have a small ceremony? It was always Lissa's dream to have an over-the-top wedding with dozens of bridesmaids and hundreds of guests and an amazing dress. Although you look lovely,' Eleanor told Lissa quickly. 'A cream suit is so elegant, and you will be able to wear it again.'

'A big wedding would take a long time to organise.' Lissa quickly made the excuse, conscious that Takis was looking at her speculatively.

'Lissa is still recovering after being seriously ill,' he explained. 'It is better that she does not have too much excitement.'

There was no danger of her getting overexcited when her fiancé had barely paid her any attention, Lissa thought wryly. She slanted a glance at Takis as they walked into the wedding room, and the glittering look he gave her made her wonder if he had read her mind.

The wedding officiant greeted them, and the civil

ceremony began. In a surprisingly short time the officiant pronounced them married. Lissa's heart missed a beat when Takis bent his head and brushed his lips over hers. It had been so long since he had kissed her, and she could not hide her response to him. Her body softened as she melted against him and parted her lips beneath his. She trembled with desire that only Takis, *her husband*, had ever made her feel.

He hesitated for a fraction of a second before his arms came around her, drawing her even closer to him so that her breasts were crushed against his chest and she felt his hard thighs through her skirt. She put her hand on his chest and felt his heart thudding as erratically as her own.

The heat of his body spread through Lissa, causing a molten warmth to pool between her legs. Instinctively, she pressed her pelvis up against his and felt the hard proof of his arousal.

He still wanted her. That at least was a start. She smiled against his mouth and heard him give a low growl as his tongue tangled with hers. The doubts she'd felt that she was doing the right thing by marrying him faded. They had never discussed one crucial aspect of their marriage, but she could feel the evidence of Takis's desire for her. Tonight was their wedding night, and she was sure he wanted to make love to her as much as she wanted him to.

A discreet cough from the officiant broke the magic. Takis lifted his mouth from Lissa's and looked faintly stunned when he realised that they had made a very public display. She heard Jace give a throaty chuckle, but Takis was grim-faced when they walked the short distance to the restaurant where they were to have lunch.

It was late in the afternoon when Eleanor and Jace left for the airport to fly back to Thessaloniki. A car collected Takis and Lissa and took them to his office building, where a helicopter was waiting on the helipad to take them to Santorini. He had explained that he owned a villa on the island.

It was a perfect location for a honeymoon, Lissa thought as the helicopter flew over the sea, which was dappled with gold in the sunset. From the air the island's half-moon shape around the rim of the caldera was clearly visible. The coastline was dramatic, with towering volcanic cliffs and beaches with unusual black sand.

'The scenery is spectacular,' she said as the helicopter dipped lower and a village with square, whitewashed houses came into view. 'The buildings with blue domed roofs are churches, aren't they?'

'Yes, they're popular with tourists who want a photo opportunity,' Takis told her. 'Santorini, and the other, smaller islands nearby were formed after a massive volcanic eruption thousands of years ago. The crater that was left after the eruption is the only sunken caldera in the world and the lagoon is said to be four hundred metres deep.'

The villa stood alone on a headland and had incredible views of the sea. Lissa had expected Takis's island home to be modern and minimalist, but the coral-pink exterior was the first of many surprises. Inside, there was colour everywhere; green and terracotta tiles on the floor, walls painted a soft cream, and in the living room there were brightly patterned cushions scattered on the sofas. A vase of vibrant yellow chrysanthemums stood in the fireplace.

'This is lovely,' she commented. 'I didn't think you were a cushions kind of person.'

'My housekeeper Efthalia is responsible for those,' Takis said drily. 'Her husband, Stelios, also works for me as a caretaker and driver. The couple live in the staff cottage.' He gave Lissa a brief smile. 'I suggest you rest before dinner. You look tired.' He moved towards the door. 'I have a couple of calls to make.'

No woman wanted to be told that she looked tired, especially on her wedding day. Or be left alone by her new husband. Lissa stared at the door after Takis closed it behind him and wondered what phone calls were so important. She was being oversensitive, she told herself. The truth was that her pregnancy did make her feel more tired. She was showing now, although she suspected that her bump was partly due to the wonderful meals the cook at the Athens house had prepared.

She climbed the stairs to the second floor of the villa and found the master bedroom, but not her luggage. A connecting door led to another bedroom, and she spied her suitcase. Her clothes had been un-packed and hung in the wardrobe. Perhaps the house-keeper assumed she would use the second bedroom as a dressing room, Lissa thought as she slipped off her shoes and lay down on the bed. She would close her eyes for five minutes and then go and drag Takis out of his study if she had to.

When she woke, it was dark outside the window and someone had switched on the bedside lamp. The nap had revived her, and she was looking for-ward to an intimate dinner with Takis. The dress she had bought for her trousseau was a scarlet sheath made of jersey silk that clung to her new curves. She ran a brush through her hair that she'd recently had trimmed into her usual jaw-length bob, applied scarlet gloss to her lips and sprayed perfume on her pulse points before going downstairs.

As she walked through the villa, Lissa was sur-prised to hear from outside the whir of rotor blades. She stepped into the garden, and her stomach swooped when she saw Takis walking towards the helicopter.

'Wait!' Her muscles unfroze and she tore across the lawn. 'Where are you going?' She cursed as she stumbled in her high heels and pulled off her shoes. 'Takis?'

He turned around slowly. His hard-boned face was expressionless, and in the darkness that seemed to press around them he was a forbidding stranger. 'I came to your room to say goodbye, but you were asleep, and I did not want to disturb you. I must return to Athens.'

'Must?' Temper beat through Lissa. 'Why?' He made no response and she said huskily, 'Explain to me how our marriage is going to work when you go out of your way to avoid me. We hardly spent any time together in Athens and I understood that you work long hours. But you brought me here to your villa, it is our wedding night and I thought…'

Her voice trailed off when he lifted his brows in that arrogant way of his that made her feel small and insignificant. She'd had a lot of practice at feeling insignificant when her grandfather had taken no interest in her, Lissa remembered bleakly.

'Why would we spend time together?' Takis sounded surprised. 'The only reason we married is so that our child will be born legitimate. We agreed that in public we will give the impression that our marriage is real, and your sister was convinced by our performance.'

'Was it a performance when you kissed me? Because it didn't feel like you were pretending.'

She had made the decision to marry him knowing that love was not involved. But she'd believed that they wanted the same things in the marriage, friendship, security for their child and yes, sex. She'd hoped that their physical compatibility would be a base on which to build their relationship, and she was sure she had not imagined the gleam of desire in Takis's eyes at their wedding.

'This conversation is pointless,' he said, stepping away from her. 'I have an early morning meeting in Athens before I'm due to fly to St Lucia to view a hotel that I am considering buying.'

'You're going to St Lucia without me?' Disappointment tore through Lissa. 'I thought we had come to Santorini for our honeymoon.' He could not have made it clearer that he was not prepared to make room for her in his life. In Athens she'd thought he was giving her time to recover from her illness, but now she realised that he regarded her as a nuisance. Would he think the same of their son when he was born? she wondered sickly.

'You have everything you need at the villa.' Frustration clipped Takis's voice. 'The staff will take care of you.' He started to walk towards the helicopter and Lissa followed him.

'When will you come back? What am I supposed to do while you are away?'

'You are on a paradise island and I'm sure you will find plenty to do. Stelios will drive you to wherever you want to go.'

Lissa noted how he avoided her first question. She watched him climb into the helicopter and wondered how she could have been so stupid as to think he might want to spend time with her or get to know her. She should have realised when he'd mostly ignored her in Athens that he wasn't interested in her. But this was not just about her.

'What about when our son is born?' she demanded. 'Will you use work as an excuse to hide in your office and ignore him too?'

Takis closed the door of the aircraft without answering her, and the *whomp-whomp* of the rotor blades grew louder. She would not cry, Lissa told herself sternly. He wasn't worth her tears, but her vision was blurred when she watched the helicopter take off. Moments later it was a beacon of light in the dark sky, taking her fragile hopes for her marriage with it.

Takis stared out of the helicopter at the night that was as black as his mood. Even as the glittering lights of Athens grew nearer he fought the temptation to instruct his pilot to fly him back to Santorini and Lissa.

When she had run across the garden wearing a sexy dress that had surely been designed to blow any red-blooded male's mind, he'd come close to forgetting that he could not have her. Could not allow himself to have her. He was determined to resist his desire for her. The damage had already been done and she was pregnant with his child, but he was not going to compound his folly by becoming more involved with her than was necessary. By letting her believe they could have anything more.

When they had arrived in Athens a month ago Lissa had still been fragile after her illness. Takis could not shake the guilt he felt that he was the reason she had almost lost her life. Her thyroid condition had become acute because of a hormonal imbalance caused by her pregnancy. He had taken a stupid risk one time when he'd made love to her and he would have to live with the repercussions.

He felt another stab of guilt as he remembered her disappointment when he'd left her behind on Santorini. *Theos*, he had not done anything to give her the idea that he'd taken her to the island for a honeymoon, he assured himself. He had kept his distance from her. Except when he had kissed her at their wedding, he recalled grimly. He had only meant it to be a token, a nod to convention when the wedding officiant had pronounced them married.

But Lissa had kissed him back and he'd been lost the instant he'd felt her mouth open beneath his. She had tasted like nectar, and he'd been powerless to fight his desire for her, which had rolled through him like a giant wave, smashing down his barriers. His wife tempted him beyond reason, which was why he had left her at the villa and instructed his pilot to fly him back to Athens.

The nagging ache in his groin mocked him. He could not give Lissa the relationship she wanted. Not even a purely physical one. And maybe she wanted more than that. He'd caught her looking at him with a wistful expression on her pretty face that had set alarm bells ringing in his head. He had married her because she and the child she carried were his responsibility. His to protect. But he felt uncomfortable when he thought of her accusation that he would ignore his son when he was born.

Takis could not imagine what it would be like to have a son. He did not know how to be a father. His own father had been a violent bully, and the only lesson Takis had learned from his childhood was how to survive. But love and tenderness? He knew nothing of those things.

When the helicopter landed at the house in Athens, he went straight to the private gym and worked out for hours in a bid to forget that this was his wedding night, and his beautiful bride was miles away. Eventually, when he was physically exhausted, he took a punishing cold shower before he crawled into bed, only for his dreams to be tormented by fantasies of having Lissa beneath him and hearing her soft cries of pleasure when he drove himself into her body.

Work was a distraction that Takis was glad to immerse himself in. He spent four days in St Lucia, finalising a deal to buy a hotel complex that would be a valuable addition to the Perseus hotel chain. To his annoyance he found himself imagining what it would be like if he had brought Lissa to the Caribbean with him and they'd honeymooned in one of the luxury lodges. If they'd made love on the private beach where the pure white sand ran down to an azure sea.

Back in Athens he spent long days at his office and when he returned to the house every evening he refused to admit that he missed Lissa being there, even though when she had shared the house with him he had avoided her as much as possible. Something that she had noticed, he thought with a stab of guilt, remembering her accusation when he'd left her at the villa that he used his work commitments as an excuse to stay away from her.

He must have imagined that Lissa's perfume lingered in the rooms at the Athens house, but he retreated to his study, which was the one room she had never entered, and tried to concentrate on financial reports for his expanding business empire to take his mind off his wife, who intruded on his thoughts with infuriating regularity.

A week passed, and another. Lissa phoned him several times, and the calls were invariably tense as she demanded to know if he intended to avoid her for the rest of her pregnancy, and beyond that, what was going to happen when their baby was born?

'I don't care if you want nothing to do with me,' she told him. 'But our son will care when he is old enough to understand that you have rejected him.'

But for the past couple of days Lissa's name had not flashed on to his phone's screen, and there had been no terse conversations, which had made Takis feel uncomfortable and guilty and unable to explain that he did not know how to be a father, or a husband for that matter. He had no role model to follow, apart from his own drunkard father.

The tenderness that he sensed Lissa hoped he would show their child, and perhaps her, simply was not in him. Maybe it had been once, but Giannis's death had made him hard and cold. It was impossible to change who he was, Takis thought, justifying his behaviour, and tried to ignore his conscience, which taunted him that he was afraid to try to change.

He flew to Naxos to visit the hotel he owned on the island and deal with an issue that needed to be resolved. His suspicions that the hotel's manager had been fiddling the accounts and moving money into a personal account proved correct. Takis fired the manager, whom he had trusted, and he was in a foul mood by the end of a frustrating day.

'I thought you should see this,' his PA said when they boarded the helicopter. Rena handed him a tabloid newspaper. 'Page three.'

Takis turned to the page and managed to restrain himself from swearing loudly when he stared at the photograph of a group of young people fooling around in a beach bar in Mykonos. He knew their type. The beautiful people, rich, bored, minor celebrities. Lissa was at the centre of the group and her smile seemed to mock him. His temper simmered as he read the caption above the photo, which had been taken the previous day.

Tycoon's new wife parties with friends in Mykonos without her husband!

Lissa's male friends were heirs to huge fortunes. They spent their time drifting around Europe's fleshpots and had probably never worked a day in their lives, Takis thought furiously. Fury shot through him. What was Lissa playing at?

He called the direct number of the manager of the Mykonos hotel, Perseus One, and learned that Lissa had checked in two days ago and was not due to leave until after the weekend.

'There has been a change of plan,' Takis told his pilot. 'You are to fly me to Mykonos before you take Rena back to Athens. I am planning to surprise my wife.'

CHAPTER ELEVEN

IT WAS DUSK when the helicopter flew low over Mykonos and landed in the grounds of the hotel. Perseus One was the first hotel Takis had bought when he'd established his hospitality business and he was proud that he had developed it to a level of breathtaking opulence demanded by its millionaire and billionaire clientele.

The marina was full of luxury motor yachts, and the hotel's casino was packed. On an island renowned for a party atmosphere, Perseus One was the place the rich and famous flocked to every Friday evening when a well-known DJ hosted an all-night party.

Takis strode into the nightclub and scanned the crowded dance floor. Lissa's pale blonde hair made her easy to spot. She was dancing with a guy who Takis recognised from the newspaper photo was Tommy Matheson—a lethargic young man whose only pursuit in life was spending his father's billions.

Lissa looked stunning. She wore the red dress she'd worn the last time Takis had seen her in Santorini. It clung to her newly voluptuous breasts and the swell of her belly where his child lay.

Anger surged through Takis when he saw how other men looked at Lissa as if they were imagining her naked. How dared they gawp at her? She was *his*. He was stunned that he felt possessive and jealous. They were not emotions he had ever experienced before or known that he was capable of feeling.

He strode across the dance floor and dropped his hand on to Lissa's shoulder, spinning her round to face him. The idiot she had been dancing with beat a hasty retreat after one look at Takis's grim face.

'What the hell are you playing at?' he demanded, raising his voice above the pounding disco music.

Lissa tilted her head and looked at him. She did not seem surprised to see him. 'I'm dancing and enjoying myself,' she said coolly. 'Is there a problem?'

He ground his teeth together. 'I have warned you before not to play games with me, *koúkla mou*.'

'Or you will do what, precisely? Take me to a pretty villa and leave me alone with no companionship and nothing to do except ask myself why I agreed to marry you?'

Her sarcasm further enraged him. 'You are carrying my child,' he snapped. 'Do I need to remind you of the reason why it was necessary for us to marry?' His eyes were drawn to the rounded swell of her stomach beneath the tight-fitting dress. Pregnancy made Lissa even more beautiful and sensual, and Takis longed to caress her gorgeous body. He clenched his fists to stop himself reaching for her. 'You are my wife and I do not appreciate you making an exhibition of yourself in public.'

Her eyes flashed, and he realised that she wasn't as calm as she made out. In fact, she was very, very angry. 'I don't understand why you should complain about me socialising with my friends. You have made it clear that you are not interested in spending time with me.'

She shrugged off his hand and carried on dancing, moving her hips sinuously to the pulse of the music and sending Takis's pulse skyrocketing. He clamped his arm around her waist. 'I want to spend time with you now. We're leaving.'

She glared at him. 'You can't *frogmarch* me out of the nightclub.'

'I think you will find that I can. Keep walking,' he advised her, 'unless you want me to carry you out of here.'

Lissa must have realised that he was serious, and she huffed out a breath as she walked beside him across the lobby. A lift whisked them up to the private suite that Takis kept for when he visited the hotel.

'Why do you object to me meeting my friends?' She rounded on him.

'I object to you courting the attention of the paparazzi.' Takis thrust the newspaper into her hand. 'A photo of my wife flirting with another man in a hotel that I own is not the sort of publicity I want for my business. You have made a fool of me.'

Lissa stared at him. 'I wasn't aware that the photo had been taken, or that it was published in the tabloids. What, do you think I wanted this to happen?' she demanded when he looked disbelieving.

'It's an occupational hazard. You attract attention.'

'You think I deliberately sought media interest?' She paled. 'Well, if that was my plan, it worked. You have been avoiding me for weeks, but when you saw my photo in the newspaper you couldn't get here fast enough so that you could criticise me, just like my grandfather used to do.'

'The situation is not the same,' Takis growled, guilt knifing him in his gut when he saw the shimmer of tears in Lissa's eyes. He guessed they were tears of anger. She was trembling with fury, and the air between them crackled with temper, hers and his.

'It's exactly the same,' she snapped. 'The only way I can get your attention is by behaving badly in public.'

'We are not in public now, and you have my undivided attention.' He did not know if he had moved or if Lissa had, but he was standing in front of her, so close that he saw her eyes darken and he heard the sudden quickening of her breaths. Takis was aware of the exact moment the spark between them caught light. He could not resist her, he didn't even try.

He bent his head and claimed her mouth, kissing

her with a desperation that on one level appalled him. He had no control when it came to this woman. An alarm rang in his mind, reminding him of the one other time he had abandoned all control when he had kissed his stepmother. This was different, he assured himself. He was not an impressionable teenager who had been convinced that his stepmother's occasional kindness to him was a sign of affection. Marina had broken his youthful heart and taught him that trust was a fool's game.

He lifted his head and stared at Lissa's lips, softly swollen from his hungry kisses. A hectic flush highlighted her cheekbones, and Takis knew she felt the tumultuous desire that was a ravenous beast inside him. He tightened his arm around her waist, bringing her body into even closer contact with his. But he tensed when he felt a rippling movement where her stomach was pressed against him.

'Was that…?' He could not disguise his shock.

Lissa smiled. 'Your son is saying hello to his daddy.'

Takis was shaken. Even at Lissa's scan, when he had seen the image of a baby on the screen, he'd felt a sense of unreality. But the movement he'd felt within her belly was not an inanimate image. It had been made by a tiny foot or fist. His son. A child he had never wanted, but nevertheless the baby deserved to have a kind and caring father. Takis did not know if he had those qualities in him. He rather doubted it. If he allowed himself to soften even a little, he might just fall apart.

He stepped back from Lissa and saw her stricken expression. Takis knew he needed to say something, but the longer the silence stretched between them the harder it became to think of anything that she might want to hear.

'Our son will be born in a few months and you had better get used to the idea,' she said in a low, intense voice that had more impact on him than if she had shouted. 'You promised to protect and love him, but I have seen no evidence that you will do so.'

'I promised to protect and provide for my child,' he corrected her. 'He will want for nothing.'

'He will want his parents to love him. Every child needs to be loved, and when they are not it causes terrible damage. I know, because my grandfather withheld his love from me, and I felt worthless. I won't allow you to make our son feel that he is un-wanted by you or a burden,' she told Takis fiercely. 'I won't allow it.'

Lissa opened her eyes and looked around at an un-familiar room before she remembered that she had spent the night in the second bedroom in Takis's private suite at the Perseus hotel. She had intended to return to her own room, but Takis had arranged for her things to be brought to his suite and she had deemed it safer not to argue with him.

They had both needed to calm down after their

blazing row over the photo that had appeared in the tabloid newspaper. Lissa forced herself to be honest about her decision to meet Tommy in Mykonos after she'd seen on a social media site that he was visiting the island, which was a popular party venue. She'd felt lonely and abandoned at the villa in Santorini. Damn it, Takis had abandoned her.

It *had* occurred to her that the paparazzi would probably be in Mykonos, keen to snap pictures of Tommy and his celebrity friends. She hadn't consciously hoped to provoke a response from Takis, but in the cold light of day she was sickened by the realisation that she'd behaved like she used to do when she had desperately sought her grandfather's attention.

Lissa ran her hand over her stomach and felt the little fluttery movements of her baby kicking. It was an incredible sensation that she had wanted to share with Takis. But his expression when he'd felt their son move had been hard to describe. He'd looked shocked, but there had been something else in his eyes. There had been fear, Lissa realised as she recalled Takis's expression. It had only been a flash of emotion before his features had reassembled into those hard angles that she found so fascinating.

Her stomach rumbled and taking care of her baby instantly became her top priority. Trying to fathom the mindset of the stranger she had married was fruitless anyway. She slipped on the silky robe that matched her negligee and stepped on to the balcony.

Her heart missed a beat when she found Takis sitting at a table spread with a variety of breakfast options.

'Come and eat,' he said, standing up and holding out a chair for her. As always, he looked gorgeous in black jeans and a cream shirt, beneath which Lissa could see the shadow of his dark chest hairs. His eyes were hidden behind sunglasses, and she wished she'd worn her shades to hide the evidence that she'd cried herself to sleep last night.

'What a view,' she murmured, wanting to distract his attention away from her. On one side of the hotel was the old port and beyond it the white cubed buildings of Mykonos town. An iconic windmill stood on the hill above the town. Lissa turned her head the other way and gave a soft sigh at the sight of the turquoise Aegean Sea sparkling in the sunshine.

'Perseus One offers the best views of the island. It's one reason why I bought the hotel.' Takis poured tea into a cup and placed it in front of Lissa. She buttered a freshly baked roll and filled a bowl with berry fruits and yogurt. Incredibly, the tensions of the previous night had eased.

'How did a boy from a poor village become one of Greece's most successful entrepreneurs?' she asked him.

He shrugged. 'It was hard at first. I was sixteen when I left my village and hitched a ride to Thessaloniki. I had no money and slept on the streets until I found work as a labourer on a construction site. I think I already told you it's where I met Jace.'

She nodded. 'The two of you became friends.'

'We shared the same drive and ambition. Jace supported his mother, but when he went to prison I looked after Iliana. It was the very least I could do after Jace had saved my life.'

He saw that Lissa was shocked. 'We were attacked by a gang. One of them attempted to stab me in the back and Jace punched him. Witnesses were paid to lie and say that Jace had started the fight. He was found guilty of grievous assault for which he was given a prison sentence.'

'That was terribly unfair. Poor Jace. Eleanor said that you and Jace are as close as brothers.'

'I guess we are.' Takis was silent for a moment and then released his breath slowly. 'I had a half-brother who died when he was a small child.'

'I'm sorry.' Lissa waited for him to add more to the tiny snippet of information about his past. But she sensed he had retreated into himself and had told her more than he'd intended.

'Soon after Jace was released from prison our fortunes changed when we won two million euros on a lottery ticket,' Takis continued. 'We shared the money equally and came to Mykonos because we'd heard that it had a great party scene. This hotel was for sale. It was derelict, but I saw its potential. I used my winnings to buy the place and turned it into the most exclusive resort on the island. At the same time I put myself through college, studying every evening, and gained a business degree.'

'You make it sound easy, but you must have worked incredibly hard,' Lissa murmured, feeling huge respect for him. The people she knew, people like Tommy Matheson, took their wealthy lifestyles for granted. They had been handed them. It's what people had believed of her too.

Takis looked at his watch. 'My helicopter pilot has just arrived from Athens and we will leave for Santorini in an hour.' His brows rose when Lissa nodded. 'I expected an argument.'

'We did enough of that last night,' she said ruefully. The state of their marriage was the elephant in the room that neither of them had addressed. There would have to be a discussion, but this morning there was a precarious connection between them that she did not want to break. 'Besides, it's too nice a day to argue.'

Takis grinned, and Lissa's breath snagged in her throat. He was impossibly sexy when he smiled. 'For once we both agree on something, *koúkla mou*,' he murmured. 'I propose we call a truce for today.'

'That's two things we agree on.' She smiled back at him and her heart lifted as she felt a little spurt of hope that they could work things out. 'Who knows, we might actually get the hang of this marriage thing.'

Lissa had assumed that the helicopter would take them directly to the villa in Santorini, and she was surprised when they landed in the grounds of a grand-looking building on the island.

'I thought you might like to see the hotel I purchased a few months ago. The building has been undergoing extensive renovations and I plan for it to open next summer,' Takis explained as he ushered her through the front door.

The hotel's main lobby was still a shell, but Lissa immediately saw its potential. Sunlight streamed through the huge windows, and the views of the caldera were breathtaking. 'I'm guessing that you can watch the sunset from this side of the hotel.'

Takis nodded. 'The rooms in the original part of the building were once caves that had been carved into the mountainside and were used to store wine. The hotel has been extended and there are fifty guest rooms and suites.'

He gave Lissa a tour of the ground floor and pointed out the various function rooms. 'As you can see, there is still a lot of work to be done inside. I asked a few interior designers to pitch a concept for the hotel and they all suggested it should be a party venue. Admittedly the designers came up with different themes, but essentially it would have the same club vibe as Perseus One in Mykonos.' He rubbed his hand over his stubbled jaw. 'I'm not sure it will work as well here.'

Lissa followed him through a set of doors and stepped on to a patio. From outside it was clear to see that the hotel had literally been carved out of the cliff in a series of terraces. A few rooms, she guessed they were the suites, had private pools. Far below, the sea was cobalt blue and made a stunning contrast to the white walls of the hotel and the vivid pink bougainvillea that tumbled over the balconies.

'Santorini has the reputation of being the most romantic of the Cyclades islands,' she said. 'I think you should make romance the theme of this hotel. Perseus One is where people go to party. But say a couple met at the nightclub in Mykonos, and a year or so later they wanted to return to Greece to get married. The Santorini hotel could offer wedding packages.'

She walked across the patio, which jutted out from the cliff so that it appeared to be floating above the sea. 'This would be a perfect setting for weddings. And you could also promote anniversary packages. People like to return to the place where they were married.'

Lissa warmed to her theme as ideas bounced around her head. 'I see Perseus One as the young, hip hotel for singles who want to have a good time and perhaps find romance. You could name this hotel Aphrodite after the goddess of love. The concept here is a little more grown-up, still fun but the decor is elegant and tranquil, and instead of a nightclub you have a restaurant that offers fine dining.'

She blushed when she realised that she had been talking non-stop. 'Sorry, I got carried away. I'm sure you have a vision for your new hotel.'

'I do now, thanks to you.' Takis took off his sunglasses and the gleam in his grey eyes made Lissa's heart flip. 'I really think you're on to something with the wedding venue suggestion. Which leads me to the reason I brought you here.'

A woman walked across the foyer towards them. 'This is Zoe,' Takis introduced her. 'Zoe, I would like you to meet my wife, Lissa.'

As they exchanged greetings Lissa immediately liked the Greek woman's friendly smile.

'Zoe is an architect,' Takis explained. 'My idea is for you to design the lobby and function rooms and Zoe will work alongside you to advise you from an architectural perspective.' He smiled at Lissa's stunned expression. 'That is, if you decide to accept the contract I am offering you.'

'Seriously?' she asked huskily. She wanted to work when the baby was older, but instead of returning to hotel management she had been thinking about starting an interior design business. 'Why have you asked me when you could hire a more qualified and experienced interior designer?'

'I was impressed with your designs at Francine's hotel when I looked through the portfolio that you had left on the desk. I also know that you recently completed an online design course and were awarded a diploma. While we were in Athens I overheard you phone your sister to tell her of your success,' Takis explained when Lissa looked puzzled. 'I wondered why you did not share your news with me.'

'I didn't think you would be interested,' she confessed. She remembered when she was a child, feeling proud that she'd won a prize at school for an art project, but when she'd rushed home to tell her grandfather, he'd told her that drawing pictures was a waste of time. She couldn't bear to have had Takis react in the same way.

'I like your idea of making the hotel a wedding venue,' Takis said. 'The name Aphrodite is a nice touch. You have the vision and artistic flare, and Zoe will help with the structural elements of your designs.'

'I would love to accept the contract.' Lissa could not hide her excitement. Ideas for the Aphrodite's lobby were already forming in her mind. 'This is an incredible opportunity for me. I won't let you down,' she promised Takis. She felt overwhelmed by his faith in her.

Maybe things were starting to fall into place, Lissa thought later when they had returned to the villa and she immediately set about turning the garden room into a design studio. She had been hurt that Takis had kept his distance after their wedding when he had left her in Santorini and returned to Athens. But earlier he had opened up a tiny chink when he'd talked about himself. She felt a connection with him because, like her, he had experienced tragedy in his life. The death of his younger brother. She only wished he'd revealed more. Why hadn't he?

Lissa frowned as she remembered his strange reaction when he'd felt the baby move inside her. He'd looked horrified, and the almost tortured expression on his face had been the same as at the ultrasound scan when Takis had stared at the baby's image on the screen. Was his reaction something to do with his brother's death?

He had not planned to have a child, Lissa reminded herself. Undoubtedly, he had been shocked when he'd learned of her pregnancy, and it was not surprising if he was taking some time to come to terms with the prospect of fatherhood. But he was the one who had insisted on marrying her and she was glad of his determination to claim his baby.

The rapport she'd felt with Takis today filled her with hope that they could make a success of their marriage. She certainly wanted to. She wanted him, Lissa admitted, feeling a sharp tug of longing in the pit of her stomach when she thought, as she so often did, of all the wonderful ways he had made love to her on the magical night they had spent together. It seemed like a lifetime ago when they had swum beneath the stars at the Pangalos hotel. She had been plagued with insecurities she'd had as a result of her grandfather's coldness towards her, but now she was going to be a mother and she had discovered that she was strong and fierce and utterly determined to protect her child from feeling rejected by his father.

She sighed as her mind returned to Takis. After their perfect night together she had crept from his bed while he was still sleeping, afraid that if she stayed she might not be able to hide how much he affected her. She had returned to Oxford and tried to get over him. But she never had. Night after lonely night she had ached for him, and the ache was worse now that he was back in her life, but not in the way she wanted.

Lissa's stomach grumbled, reminding her that it was time she fed her baby. She had asked the house-keeper to make moussaka for dinner because it was Takis's favourite. But when she went into the dining room she was surprised to see only one place had been set on the table.

Efthalia came in, carrying a casserole dish. 'Kyrios Samaras told me that he would not be stay-ing for dinner,' she explained.

With a sinking heart and a sickening sense of déjà vu, Lissa looked out of the window and saw the pilot climb into the helicopter. Was Takis planning to abandon her once more? Disappointment brought tears to her eyes, but she blinked them away as anger swept through her in a hot tide of temper. She would not let Takis do this to her. To their baby.

She hurried across the hallway and burst into his study. 'You have asked me several times if I was playing games, even though I've always been hon-est and open with you. Now I'm asking you the same question.' She glared at him. 'You had better have a good explanation for why you are leaving me and our baby again.'

CHAPTER TWELVE

TAKIS CLOSED HIS laptop case with a decisive snap, but Lissa noted that he evaded eye contact with her. 'I am returning to Athens because it is where my business is based.'

'You could work remotely from the villa just as easily as if you were in your office.'

'Not everything can be managed online. I prefer to meet my executive team face to face.'

'You are making excuses.' She bit her lip. 'I thought you would stay in Santorini and we would both be involved with the plans for the refurbishment of the Aphrodite.'

'You don't need me here. I trust that you will do a good job, and you can discuss your design ideas with Zoe.' He started to walk towards the door, but Lissa planted herself firmly in front of him. 'You said you were bored and had nothing to do. Now you have the hotel project to occupy you.'

'Is that why you gave me the contract?' She felt sick with the realisation that he had been humouring her. That he did not really have any faith in her, he was merely trying to find a way to amuse her while he was gone. The pleasure she'd felt that he had chosen her to design the Aphrodite evaporated, leaving anger and hurt in its place. 'I am not a child who you need to keep entertained.'

'You are acting like one. I gave you the design contract because I like your ideas. I need to be in Athens, but you will remain here in Santorini to oversee the work on the Aphrodite.' Frustration edged into his voice. But there was something else too that Lissa didn't quite recognise. Desperation. And it bolstered her.

'The real reason you're leaving is because it suits you for us to live apart,' Lissa asserted as he stepped past her. 'What are you afraid of, Takis?'

He turned in the doorway and frowned at her. 'What do you mean? I'm not afraid of anything.'

'I think you are lying.' She should have quailed at the glowering look he sent her, but temper won over common sense, which urged her to remove herself from the conversation and the room with her dignity intact. 'I think you are afraid of me.'

He walked back to her. Not walked, *stalked* like a wolf hunting down its prey, Lissa thought when he smiled, showing his white teeth. But he did not smile with his eyes, and his hard gaze bored into her. 'Why would I be afraid of you, *koúkla mou*?' he asked, his voice deceptively soft, but she heard the bite behind it.

Lissa did not know what came over her then. Perhaps it was the memory of the way he had kissed her at their wedding with a hungry passion that had lit a flame inside her. Or how he'd kissed her the previous night in Mykonos and the taste of him lingered on her lips still.

Maybe it was simply because she wanted to, she decided as she stood on tiptoe and balanced herself by putting her hands on his shoulders. 'I think you are afraid of this,' she whispered against his mouth, and then she kissed him.

He stiffened and clamped his hands over hers as if he intended to pull her away from him. His mouth was an inflexible line, and Lissa was sure she had lost whatever silly battle she had started. He didn't want her, and his rejection was nothing new, she thought bleakly. She was an expert at being rejected. She dipped her tongue into his mouth, wanting one last taste of him, and to her amazement he gave a low growl from deep in his throat. The sound was shockingly erotic and raw with sexual need.

He dropped his hands and wrapped his arms around her, hauling her up against his whipcord body. His lips moved over hers as he took control of the kiss and the fire inside Lissa became an inferno. She felt Takis shake and knew that she was shaking too. When she finally tore her mouth from his and stepped away from him, his eyes glittered, and he looked stunned.

'Damn you,' he said thickly. 'What do you want from me, Lissa?'

'I want a proper marriage.' The words burst from her. 'When you insisted that we should marry for the sake of our baby, what did you envisage our relationship would be like? You must have thought about it,' she said when he frowned. 'Is your plan for us to always live apart? You in Athens and me here in the villa? And what will happen when our son is born? Will you ignore him as you do me? Because if that is your plan, to be an absent father like you are an absent husband, it's not good enough.'

'The baby is not here yet,' Takis said icily. There was no sign in his cold eyes of the hot desire that had blazed there moments ago.

'We should use the time before he arrives to learn more about each other and discuss how we want to be parents. But how can we do that if you keep running away?'

'I am not *running away*,' he said furiously.

'Why don't you want to spend time with me?' Her voice rose with the hurt and anger she could not hide. 'I am the mother of your child. Don't you want to know what kind of mother I will be, or don't you care?'

'*Theos*, Lissa.' He raked his hand through his hair. 'What do you want from me?' he repeated harshly.

'I want to know what kind of father you will be. What kind of husband, and whether you actually want to be married to me—because that is not at all clear.'

She swallowed as a thought occurred to her. 'You left me to spend my wedding night alone after you dumped me here. Is that because you have other interests in Athens besides your business?'

Takis stared at her and she saw the exact moment he grasped her meaning. He looked outraged. 'Do you think I have a mistress in Athens?'

'I don't know what to think,' she said flatly. 'I might not have much experience of these things, of men, but I know you are a highly sensual man, and we are not...' She flushed. 'You are not satisfying your desire with me.'

'So it stands to reason that I have another woman? I did not *dump* you at the villa,' he gritted. 'I have provided—'

'So you keep reminding me,' she cut him off. 'But our baby will need more than material things. He will need a father who comforts him in the night and reads him stories. A hands-on father, not one who lives miles away and bangs on about how he provides and protects, when as far as I am concerned you do neither.'

He stepped closer to her, a dangerous look in his eyes that made her tremble, but with excitement, not fear. Takis seemed dumbfounded that she had questioned him, but it was vital for her to discover if he would be a caring father or if he would treat their son with the indifference her grandfather had treated her.

Lissa had never really understood why Pappoús had disliked her, and she had certainly never dared to ask him. But for the first time in her life she was standing up for herself and fighting for what she wanted, for the marriage she wanted, and it felt good.

'Is this another attempt to get my attention?' Takis ground out. He was breathing hard and his eyes were like a terrible storm, dark and ominous. This was the man behind the mask, Lissa realised with a jolt. Takis was not the unemotional rock of granite that he wanted her to believe. His emotions were exposed, stark and savage on his face. She understood that he hoped if he looked menacing she would back down. She did not fully understand why he still needed to keep her at arm's length, but she had come this far, and retreat was not an option.

She met his tormented gaze boldly. 'If it is, what are you going to do about it?'

Takis hauled Lissa into his arms and slammed his mouth down on hers. He was willing to do anything to stop her asking questions that he did not know how to answer. He kissed her to prevent her from challenging him in a fierce voice and with an even fiercer expression on her face as she demanded to know what kind of father he planned on being.

He hadn't planned any of this. He hadn't wanted a child, or a wife, let alone a wife who forced him to ask himself the same questions she had flung at him. And he still did not know the answers. All he knew was that he wanted her beneath him, on top of him, any which way as long as he could bury himself in her molten heat.

He roamed his hands over her body, discovering her round curves, which distracted him constantly. Even when he'd removed himself to Athens after their wedding—so that he was on the pulse of his business, he assured himself, not because he had been *running away*—Lissa had been a distraction. He had spent his nights in a fury of sexual frustration, but he'd told himself it would pass. If he kept away from her, his desire for her would fade. And then he'd seen the photo of her in the newspaper and he'd seized the excuse to rush to Mykonos to claim his wife.

'What kind of marriage do *you* want?' he asked when he finally lifted his mouth from hers, but kept her body clamped against him. The rock-hard proof of his arousal straining beneath his trousers mocked his belief that he had any control where Lissa was concerned. And he no longer cared that she knew the effect she had on him when she smiled her beautiful smile that tugged on something deep inside him.

'I want you,' she said simply.

Her honesty was his undoing and demanded that he be honest with himself. He could not fight his need for her. Takis had prided himself on never needing anyone, but pride was a lonely bedfellow, and he was tired of always being alone.

'Do you want me to do this?' he asked thickly

as he slanted his mouth over hers again and kissed her with fierce passion. He felt her tremble as he trailed his lips down her neck and pressed his mouth against the pulse that was beating erratically at the base of her throat.

His hands trembled with need as he unfastened the buttons on her blouse and traced his finger over her sheer, pale pink bra. 'Pretty,' he growled. Her blouse fell to the floor, followed by her bra, and Takis groaned as her breasts spilled into his hands. 'Prettier,' he said thickly as he rubbed his thumb pads over her dusky pink nipples and felt them swell and harden to his touch.

He looked into her eyes, which were deep blue pools, deep enough to drown in. She made him think of summer skies and laughter, and for the first time since he was a teenager he wondered if there was hope for him. He wanted to step out of the darkness into Lissa's golden light.

Her skirt was made of a stretchy material that moulded the firm swell of her pregnant stomach. Takis was fascinated by her new shape, her sensual roundness where once she had been angular, and he could not get enough of her voluptuous breasts. He tugged her skirt off and his eyes roamed over her lace panties.

'Are you sure?' he asked her. He did not know how he'd bear it if she had changed her mind, but he needed to give her the chance to reconsider, because if he made love to her there would be no going back. She would be his. He would no longer be able to stay away.

'I'm sure,' she murmured.

His heart thudded as he pulled her knickers off and lifted her up, sitting her on the edge of his desk. He cupped her breasts in his hands and bent his head to take one rosy nipple into his mouth. She gasped as he suckled her, leaning back and supporting herself with her hands on the desk so that her body arched, and her breasts were presented to him like ripe, round peaches that he feasted on hungrily.

Her guttural moans ran right through him, all the way down to his shaft, and made him harden even more. His body was impatient, but it wasn't surprising for he had not done this for months, not since the night he'd spent with Lissa at the Pangalos hotel. But even though he felt like he might explode, he was determined to control his hunger until he'd satisfied hers.

Takis dropped to his knees and pushed her legs apart so that he could trace his lips along her inner thigh. She made another of those husky moans as he licked her moist opening and pushed his tongue inside her. He felt her fingers slide into his hair and shape his skull while he caressed her intimately until she was panting, and he knew she was close to climaxing.

'I want you,' she told him in that fierce way of hers that tugged on something inside him. Her eyes were huge and dark with desire and her blonde hair curled against her flushed cheeks. She was the most beautiful thing he had ever seen, and he did not deserve her beauty, her smile. Takis knew it, but he could not help himself. He unzipped his trousers and freed his erection. He was harder than he had ever been, and he needed her now. He positioned himself between her thighs and pressed forward, sliding into her with a smooth thrust that drew a gasp from her.

'Am I hurting you?' he muttered, his mouth against her neck.

'No, it's just been a while since we last did this.'

He registered her words and knew he should feel appalled by the possessiveness that thundered through him, but instead he felt strangely humbled that she was his and his alone. He pulled back almost completely and then thrust again, deep into her velvet heat, into the sweet embrace of her femininity, and it felt like he'd come home at last.

Lissa wrapped her legs around his hips as he began to move, carefully at first, but when he sensed that her urgency was as great as his, he increased his pace and the intensity of his thrusts, taking them both higher. It couldn't last, but he gritted his teeth and fought for control. His hands gripped the edge of the desk and he felt the moment she tensed.

'Takis…' She sobbed his name as he drove into her again and felt her shatter around him. And he came almost instantly, his orgasm sweeping through him so that he shuddered with the pleasure of it that had never been this intense with any other woman.

After a long time he withdrew from her and adjusted his clothes. 'Are you all right? The baby...'

'We are both fine,' Lissa assured him softly.

There was a whole great mess in his head that he would have to face sometime, Takis acknowledged. But not now. He did not want to think of all those questions of Lissa's that needed answers. Tonight he simply wanted to be with her, and so he swept her up into his arms and carried her up to his bed, where he made love to her again and again until they collapsed exhausted in each other's arms.

Lissa fell asleep with her head resting on his chest. Takis placed his hand on her stomach, and his heart stood still when he felt the baby kick. He swallowed hard, unable to assimilate the feelings that stirred inside him. Was this tenderness, this ache beneath his breastbone when he imagined his son? He wished he could be a better man than he knew he was and a better father than the one he was afraid he would be.

'Who is Giannis?'

Takis turned his head on the pillow and met Lissa's cornflower-blue gaze. He had woken to a sense of contentment that he hadn't felt for months. Perhaps even years. But he tensed when she said, 'You were dreaming and called out the name Giannis.'

She rolled on to her side and propped herself up on her elbow, drawing the sheet over her ripe breasts that Takis would admit he was addicted to touching.

'I apologise if I disturbed you. I occasionally have nightmares.' He tried to sound casual, hoping that Lissa would not pursue the matter. But he should have known it was an unrealistic hope. He was learning that his wife was tenacious as well as fierce.

'What are your nightmares about?'

Takis exhaled deeply. 'Giannis was my younger brother.' He answered her first question. 'Half-brother, technically. We had the same father but different mothers.'

'I remember you said that your brother died when he was a child. Was he ill?'

'No.' Takis swung his legs over the side of the bed and pulled on his trousers before walking over to stand by the window. Outside it was another beautiful day in Santorini, with the sun shining in an azure sky on to the turquoise sea below. But in his mind he pictured the barren grey mountains around his village, the scrubby grass that had sustained his father's herd of goats. The blackened, charred remains of the place he had called home, although it had never been one. Not in the way the villa felt like home, but he suspected that might have something to do with the fact Lissa was here.

'There was a fire. Giannis was killed in a house fire along with my father and stepmother.'

'How terrible!' Lissa's voice was very soft. 'How did it start? A house doesn't simply burst into flames,' she said when he swung round from the window and stared at her.

'It was thought that my father dropped a smouldering cigarette on to the sofa before he fell asleep. No doubt he was drunk.' Takis shoved his hands into his pockets and clenched them into fists. 'His body was discovered by the front door so it's assumed he must have tried to escape. My stepmother and brother were asleep upstairs. The fire was ferocious and swept through the house. They didn't stand a chance.'

Lissa's eyes were fixed on him. 'You were the only one of your family to survive. Oh, Takis.'

He could not bear her sympathy. He did not deserve it. But suddenly he could not bear the secret shame that had weighed on him since he was sixteen. He knew if he told Lissa the truth, the gentle expression in her eyes would turn to disgust. Only perhaps then she would understand why she and their son were better off without him.

'I was not in the house. I had abandoned my brother when I left the village a few days before the fire.'

Her brow wrinkled in a tiny frown. 'You didn't abandon him if he was with his parents.'

Takis snorted. 'My father was a bully with a filthy temper and a habit of using his belt on me. As for my stepmother, Marina was much younger than my father. She was barely eighteen when she gave birth to my half-brother. I was eleven when Giannis was born. He was the cutest baby and toddler. When he grew older, he was my shadow. I was the person he wanted if he grazed his knee.' Takis swallowed. 'He adored me, and I him. But I betrayed his faith in me. I left him when he was five years old and I never saw him again.'

Lissa slid out of bed and wrapped the sheet around her to cover her stomach wherein lay another innocent little boy, who had no knowledge of his father's cowardice, Takis brooded, conscious of a terrible ache in his chest.

'Why did you leave?' she asked.

He wondered why he was still telling her any of it. Perhaps it was so that she would stop looking at him with a light in her eyes as if she saw something in him, some goodness that he knew did not exist.

'My stepmother tried to seduce me,' he said tautly. 'I was sixteen and thought I was in love with her. I convinced myself that she loved me, and so I kissed her. Marina had known that I was planning to leave the village and go to the city to look for work and make a better life. She wanted me to take her and Giannis along, and she threatened to tell my father that I had tried to force myself on her if I refused.'

He turned his head towards the window once again and the stunning view from his villa. Other men envied him his wealth and success, but he was empty inside, and until he'd met Lissa that emptiness hadn't bothered him overmuch.

'I felt a fool when I realised that Marina had been stringing me along,' he admitted rawly. 'My teenage pride was crushed, and I couldn't bear to see her again knowing she had been laughing at me. So that night I left.'

He sensed that Lissa had crossed the room to stand beside him, but he could not bring himself to look at her. 'I thought that Giannis would be safe. My father had some fondness for him and did not beat him. I had the crazy idea that I would find work, save some money and go back for Giannis when I could support him.'

Grief caught in his throat. 'I promised him that I would go back for him. He begged me not to leave him, but I went anyway, and he died in the fire.'

'You couldn't have known what would happen. No one can see the future,' Lissa said gently.

'You don't understand,' he ground out, his shame a savage torment that had never left him in all these years. 'I was in a temper because of what my step-mother had done. I left because I wanted to show her that I did not care about her, like she didn't care about me.'

Takis made himself turn around to face the con-demnation that he was certain would be in Lissa's gaze. But there were tears in her eyes, not judgement.

'What else could you have done but leave?' she asked quietly. 'You were sixteen. A boy not yet fully a man, and your stepmother took advantage of you. If you had somehow managed to take her and Giannis away with you, what kind of life would they have had? You told me that you slept on the streets when you first arrived in the city. How could you have taken care of a child when you lived rough and begged for food?'

She stepped closer and put her hand on his chest. 'The fire was a terrible twist of fate, but it was not your fault that Marina and Giannis died. For twenty years you have believed you were to blame for an accident that you couldn't have prevented. Isn't it time you learned to forgive yourself, for our son's sake if nothing else?'

Takis stared at her and realised with a jolt of shock that her tears were for him. 'You asked me what kind of father I will be. My only experience of a father was the monstrous man who failed me every day of my childhood. I wasn't there for my brother when he needed me. I failed Giannis. You can see there is a pattern here,' he said harshly. 'There is no guarantee that I will not fail my own child.'

'I don't believe that,' Lissa said softly. 'I don't believe that you are in any way like your father.'

'How can you be sure? You do not know me.'

'Then let me know you.' She stood in front of him and held his gaze, that fierce light that he was beginning to recognise was a part of her shining in her eyes. 'Stay here with me so that we can learn about each other, for our son's sake.'

CHAPTER THIRTEEN

TAKIS STAYED BECAUSE he could not bring himself to leave her. This woman who confounded him and amazed him more with every day that he learned something new about her. His wife was wise, Takis discovered. She understood there was a darkness inside him, and bit by bit he started to open up to her.

They lived at the villa, but not separately like when they had lived in the house in Athens before they'd married. Takis shared his bed with Lissa, ate his meals with her and spent all his time with her. They talked and laughed and made love endlessly, but he still could not get enough of her. Most days he worked in his study for a few hours and Lissa went into her design studio and made plans for the Aphrodite hotel.

Occasionally Takis had reason to go to his office in Athens, but he always returned in the evening, and when he climbed out of the helicopter and watched Lissa hurry across the garden to meet him it was like the first time he had ever seen her. That kick in his gut and the feeling that his life would never be the same again. Which, of course, it wouldn't.

Soon Lissa was in the third trimester of her pregnancy and before long Takis would have a son. He did not know how he felt about that. He still avoided thinking about his imminent fatherhood or what kind of father he would be.

'Life is about choices,' Lissa told him. 'I don't believe we are born with our destiny mapped out in advance. We control our own destinies, as you did when you chose not to be a goat herder in a poor village and instead built a business empire. Just because your father was a brute, it doesn't mean that you will be like him.'

Takis wanted to believe her, but sometimes in the middle of the night, when he lay in bed with Lissa curled up asleep beside him and felt his baby kick, he saw Giannis's face and heard the little boy's sobs. *'Don't leave me!'* It occurred to Takis that if he maintained a distance from his son when he was born, the child would not love him as Giannis had loved him, and so would not be devastated if his father failed him.

Takis set his complicated thoughts aside as he walked into the villa. This evening he and Lissa were to host a party to celebrate the completion of the refurbished Aphrodite hotel. His wife was very talented and she had done an amazing job. As he'd known she would. And Takis had shamelessly used his contacts to make sure everyone else knew it too. The guest list read like a who's who of Europe's social elite.

His meeting in Athens had overrun so he'd changed into a tuxedo before the helicopter had brought him back to Santorini.

Lissa was in their bedroom. Takis halted in the doorway, transfixed when she turned towards him. 'You look…' Words failed him.

'Like a whale?' she said drily, but Takis heard uncertainty in her voice and something inside him cracked.

'Beautiful,' he growled. She looked like a goddess in a gold floor-length gown. The off-the-shoulder bodice framed her ripe, round breasts. Her dress was made of some sort of shimmery material that skimmed over the big mound of her stomach.

Takis had noticed that she often touched her baby bump, and now she placed her hands on her belly in a protective gesture that made him want to fall to his knees and worship her. His child's mother would never abandon her son like Takis's mother had abandoned him. Like he had abandoned his brother. His son would always be loved.

He was aware of a host of emotions that he did not want to define. Because he was afraid, whispered a voice inside his head.

'You look incredible,' he told her as he walked over to her and drew her into his arms. '*I ómorfi gynaíka mou*. My beautiful wife.'

* * *

Fireworks exploded inside Lissa when Takis slanted his mouth over hers and kissed her. There was passion in his kiss but also a beguiling tenderness that dismantled the defences she tried to maintain around her heart to protect it from her husband. To protect herself from falling in love with him. She suspected that she was not doing very well on that score.

He groaned and pulled her against his whipcord body, as close as her swollen belly would allow. But Lissa jolted back to reality and regretfully broke the kiss.

'We can't,' she gasped, snatching air into her lungs. Takis's eyes gleamed like molten steel as he stared down at her. 'We can't be late for the party,' she reminded him. 'It is an important night for you, the opening of the tenth hotel in the Perseus chain.'

His chest heaved as he released a ragged breath. 'Tonight is *your* night to shine when your designs are unveiled. As badly as I want to make love to you, and I do, desperately, I will make myself wait for a few hours. You deserve your time in the spotlight and the accolades for your work that I know you will receive.'

He reached inside his jacket and withdrew a narrow box, which he opened to reveal an exquisite necklace and drop earrings made of rose gold and set with white diamonds.

Lissa's eyes widened when he held the box out to her. 'I can't accept...'

'Please. I had them made for you.'

Swallowing hard, she turned towards the mirror and attached the earrings to her lobes while Takis stood behind her and fastened the necklace around her throat.

'They're dazzling,' she whispered, tracing her finger over the diamonds sparkling on her décolletage. The jewellery was beautiful, but it was the expression in Takis's eyes, a softness that had not been there before, that made Lissa's heart turn over.

'You will dazzle our guests,' he said thickly. 'While we are at the party I will be imagining you wearing the diamonds and nothing else, which is exactly what will happen later tonight.' He slid his arms around her waist and placed his hands on her stomach just as the baby gave a hard kick.

His expression shifted and for a moment there was a look of such intense pain on his face that Lissa caught her breath. Takis had appointed one of the top obstetricians in the country to oversee her pregnancy, and he paid for Dr Papoulis to fly to Santorini every week for the antenatal appointments. But she still did not really know how he felt about becoming a father, or how he felt about her, for that matter.

They had grown closer since he'd moved into the villa and their marriage was working out better than Lissa had dared hope. But something was missing. Love was missing. She tried to convince herself that what she had with Takis, friendship, mutual respect and their physical compatibility, was enough. But it did not feel enough.

Sometimes she wondered if she was destined to spend her life longing to be loved, and it hurt because she had so much love inside her to give. She wondered what would happen if she were brave enough to tell Takis of her feelings for him. But if she did, and he did not feel the same way about her, it would drive him away.

Takis stepped away from her and picked up her wrap from the bed. 'We should go,' he murmured as he handed it to her, 'or we will be late.'

He drove them along the winding coast road to the hotel. Butterflies leapt in Lissa's stomach when she stood with Takis in the Aphrodite's opulent lobby to greet the guests. She had hoped that her dramatic designs would make an impact when people entered the hotel, and the favourable comments that she overheard seemed to indicate that she'd pulled it off.

'I am proud of my hotel and incredibly proud of you,' Takis told her later in the evening when he found her in the wedding room. 'You did not need to feel nervous. Everyone is blown away by your creation of a unique venue that has an ambiance that is both welcoming and unashamedly luxurious.'

'How did you know I was nervous?' she asked.

'I know you, *koúkla mou*,' he said softly. 'There

is an English expression, you wear your heart on
your sleeve.'

Lissa hoped he could not really tell everything
that she was thinking and feeling. For the first time
ever, she was glad to be interrupted by a journalist,
who came into the room and asked for an interview.
It helped that the journalist was not a member of the
paparazzi and worked for a prestigious interior design magazine.

'What was your inspiration for the wedding room
and the stunning terrace where open-air weddings
can take place?' the journalist asked.

'Since I was a little girl, I imagined getting married in a beautiful, romantic setting, and I wanted to
create a fairy-tale venue where brides and grooms
can have a truly magical wedding of their dreams.'

'You must have wished that the Aphrodite had
been finished in time for your own wedding,' the
journalist commented.

Lissa felt Takis's gaze on her and wondered if he
was remembering the functional room in the civic
hall where they had married purely because she had
conceived his child. She needed to remember the
reason why he had married her. 'A wedding is special wherever it takes place,' she said to the journalist, hoping she sounded convincing.

Those butterflies inside her started fluttering
again when Takis drove the car away from the hotel
at the end of the evening. Although he told her she
was beautiful, she felt insecure about her pregnant

body. When they walked into the villa he swept her into his arms and carried her up the stairs to the bedroom, ignoring her pleas to put her down because she weighed a ton.

'Do you not see how beautiful you are?' he murmured as he freed her from the bodice of her dress and made a feral sound in his throat as he cradled her bare breasts in his hands. He tugged her dress down over her stomach so that it slid to the floor, leaving her in her tiny, lace knickers and the diamond necklace sparkling at her throat.

She stared at their reflections in the mirror. His tanned hands cupped her pale breasts, and streaks of dull colour ran along his cheekbones. He rubbed his thumb pads over her nipples until they were pebble-hard and rosy pink.

'You are a goddess. *My* goddess,' Takis told her in an unsteady voice that clutched at her heart. He stripped off his clothes with an urgency that thrilled her, and then he sat her on the edge of the bed and sank to his knees in front of her. He pushed her thighs apart and worshipped her with his tongue and his clever fingers until she sobbed his name.

'Lissa *mou*.' He murmured her name like a prayer as he slowly eased his swollen length inside her. She gasped as he filled her, and he hesitated and withdrew a little way.

'Am I hurting you?' His gentle concern curled around her heart.

'Only when you stop,' she muttered as she

wrapped her legs around his hips to bring her pelvis flush with his.

He laughed softly. 'I have no intention of stopping until you scream my name, *koúkla mou*.'

It was the sweetest threat Lissa had ever heard and she gloried in his fierce possession as he thrust deep, over and over again. She could deny him nothing. She was conscious only of Takis driving into her, taking her higher, and then holding her there at the edge for timeless seconds. He slipped his hand between their bodies and gave a clever twist of his fingers, and his name left her lips on a sharp cry as she shattered.

He hadn't finished with her and built her up again with his skilful caresses so that she climaxed twice more. Only then, when she was flushed with ecstasy and utterly replete, did he take his own pleasure with a hard thrust that tore a groan from his throat.

Afterwards he lifted himself off her and cradled her against his chest. Lissa loved the warm afterglow as much as she loved the amazing sex, but as she hovered on the edge of sleep a thought niggled in her mind. Takis had seemed to enjoy their lovemaking, but he had been different tonight, more controlled. They had just shared the most intimate moments that two people could experience, but despite their physical closeness he was still unreachable.

The baby was due in eight weeks, and Takis was concerned about Lissa flying in the helicopter and insisted on them returning to Athens to be closer to the private maternity hospital where she was booked to give birth. He had bought the house that he'd previously leased, and Lissa spent happy hours designing and overseeing the decoration of the nursery. She had been worried that Takis might spend hours in his study, as he had done in the past, but the close relationship that had developed between them in Santorini continued to flourish.

He had encouraged Lissa to set up her own interior design business. 'There is no need for you to work and I know you want to be a full-time mother for a while, but you are amazingly talented, and you could take on design contracts when the baby is a bit older, if you want to.'

Lissa had glowed with pride at Takis's praise. For a long time she had believed her grandfather when he had told her that she would never be good at anything, even after his death. But she had proved to herself that she was not worthless. She was no longer the person who had hidden her insecurity behind a party girl image that had never been the real her. She was a woman growing in self-confidence, a wife, and soon to be a mother.

The next step on her journey to what she hoped would be her very own happy-ever-after was to be honest with Takis about how she felt about him. Once, she would have been too afraid of rejection to contemplate such a daring step. But she had a good reason to overcome her fear, Lissa thought when her son kicked so hard against her ribcage that she caught her breath. Even if Takis did not love her, she had to know if he would love their baby. If he could love their baby.

All these thoughts came to her early one morning when the new dawn made the world seem full of possibilities. And because she had become brave, and before her nerve failed her, she rolled on to her side in the bed, which was no easy task when her big belly was cumbersome, and her eyes met Takis's sleepy gaze.

'Kaliméra, koúkla mou.' His sexy smile almost stole her the words she was about to speak.

'I need to tell you something. I'm falling in love with you.'

Takis froze and his gut twisted into a knot of fear. Love had ripped his heart out and left a void in his chest ever since he had thrown a handful of earth on to Giannis's coffin. He didn't have any love to give. How had he let this happen, let things get this far?

'Take my advice and don't,' he told Lissa curtly.

She dropped her hand from his chest, and he hated the look of hurt on her face, hated that he was the cause of it.

'Why complicate things?' He made his voice softer, realising that he needed to reassure her of his commitment. 'We have become good friends as well as good lovers. I respect you and I admire your talent. I'm hoping that when the baby is older, you will accept a position with my Perseus hotel chain as an interior design consultant.'

He lifted his hand to smooth her long fringe off her face and felt the knot inside him tighten when she turned her head away, but not before he'd glimpsed the disappointment in her eyes. Disappointment with him. She shifted across to her side of the bed. It was a very big bed, and the chasm that he sensed had opened up between him and Lissa was widening by the second. But what was he to do? Takis asked himself. He had not asked her to fall in love with him. The idea of it appalled him. Lissa deserved better. He was dead inside, and he couldn't change. Maybe he did not want to change, suggested a snide little voice inside him. Maybe he was too much of a coward to try.

'We will create a family for our son like the happy family you once had,' he sought to reassure her. Takis had no experience of a happy family, but he knew family was important to Lissa and he was prepared to promise anything to see that light in her eyes again. 'It is my responsibility to make a success of our marriage and I will not fail to do the best for our son and for you.'

Lissa nodded as she got up out of the bed, but she did not look at him. He wondered if that could be enough for her.

* * *

Over the next two weeks Takis did his best to prove that he was committed to their marriage, even if he could not give Lissa the romantic dream she hoped for. Thankfully, she had not said anything more about her feelings for him. That morning, when she'd dropped a boulder into the still pool of their relationship, he had handled it badly, he acknowledged. She had locked herself in the bathroom for a worryingly long time, eventually emerging with flushed cheeks—from having had a bath, she'd told him—and suspiciously bright eyes that neither of them mentioned.

They both tried to carry on as if nothing had happened, but he felt edgy and he sensed that Lissa had withdrawn from him. One Saturday, Takis suggested a trip to the Acropolis Museum. They spent a few hours wandering around the exhibition halls before climbing the steep path and steps up to the top of the Acropolis hill to wander around the breathtaking Parthenon, built as a temple dedicated to the goddess Athena.

'What an incredible view,' Lissa murmured as they stood and looked at the city spread out before them. She rubbed her lower back and Takis frowned when he saw her wince.

'Are you in pain?' He led her over to a bench. 'Sit for a while. We shouldn't have spent so long in the museum. Too much standing is not good for you.'

'A bit of backache is normal at this stage of my

pregnancy.' She took a sharp breath. 'I've been having some of the practice contractions that the obstetrician said might happen.'

'*Theós!* Why did you not tell me before we climbed to the top of the hill?' Fear greater than he had ever felt before made Takis's heart clench.

'I'm fine.' Lissa focused on her breathing, like the midwife at the antenatal classes had told her. She'd woken with mild backache that morning but hadn't paid much attention to what had been no more than a niggle. When Takis had suggested visiting the museum her foolish heart had leapt at the chance to spend time with him away from the house, which had felt claustrophobic since she'd mentioned the L word.

His horrified expression would have almost been funny if it hadn't made her want to weep. Pride had got her into the bathroom before she'd let her tears fall, and pride had made her stick a plaster over her wounded heart and carry on as if she did not feel utterly broken by his rejection.

'We must go home,' Takis said now in a tense voice. She couldn't work out if he was annoyed or concerned. She let him help her to her feet and was glad of his hand beneath her elbow when a pain shot across her stomach. By the time they had walked back down the hill and climbed into the car, the tightening sensations were happening with alarming regularity. Her labour could not have started six weeks early, Lissa tried to reassure herself. But the next contraction was so intense that she gave a cry.

'Takis…' She hesitated. 'I think the baby is coming.'

He swore and pulled out his phone to call the maternity hospital. 'They know we are on our way,' he told her after he'd instructed the chauffeur to drive faster.

'It might be a false alarm.' Lissa gritted her teeth as another sharp pain tore through her.

'Mr Papoulis and his obstetrics team are preparing for you to give birth.'

Takis had never seemed so remote but for once Lissa wasn't thinking about him. 'I'm scared,' she said on a sob. 'It's too early for the baby to be born.'

Their son didn't think so. She needed an emergency Caesarean. Lissa's blood pressure was soaring, and the baby was in distress, so she was rushed into Theatre and given an epidural anaesthetic. Everything became a frightening blur of bright lights and urgent voices from medical staff dressed in green operating gowns.

But then Takis appeared beside the trolley where she was lying. His eyes locked with hers as he clasped her hand in his strong fingers, and she clung to him as if he were a lifeline. She could not see over the screen that had been put across her stomach, but Takis suddenly gripped her hand tighter. *'He's here.* The baby has been born.'

'Is he all right?' Lissa asked fearfully. The silence seemed to last for an eternity before she heard a shrill cry as the baby took his first breath. Tears streamed down her face when a nurse placed the tiny infant on her chest for a few moments, but then he was wrapped up in blanket ready to be whisked away to the neonatal unit.

'His name is Elias,' Lissa told her nurse, who was writing the labels to go around the baby's fragile wrist and ankle. She understood that her baby would need special care, but her arms ached to hold him, and her heart ached for love that she hoped her son would feel for her. Love that her husband could not or would not give her.

Takis stared at his baby son lying in the incubator with wires and tubes attached to his tiny body. It was impossible to believe that this scrap of humanity would survive. He blamed himself for Elias's premature birth. Lissa should have been resting, not traipsing around a museum. It was he who had not been able to give her the love she deserved. Who had suggested they leave the confines of their home to escape the emotions left unspoken, but which hung in the air. He was sure that was the reason she had gone into early labour.

His heart clenched. The baby had a mass of dark hair and reminded him of Giannis. *Theos!* Takis had not wanted a child, but his son was here, fragile and terrifyingly vulnerable. He had promised that he would protect his son and provide for him, and he would gladly do both. But more than that? He remembered how Lissa had looked at him and said fiercely, 'You have to love our child.'

Love, that most unstable of emotions that risked pain and heartbreak. He did not want to take the risk and feel the pain of loss. He dared not love his little son.

'What kind of father will you be?' Lissa had asked him. Now he had the answer. Elias's father was a coward, and if Lissa knew the truth, no doubt the light in her eyes that shone so brightly when she looked at him, that light that made him want to be a better man, would dim.

CHAPTER FOURTEEN

LISSA EXPERIENCED A rollercoaster of emotions in the first tense week after she'd given birth prematurely. She felt a mixture of joy and fear when she looked at her tiny baby in an incubator. But Elias was a fighter and day by day he continued to thrive.

She stayed in the hospital with the baby for a further three weeks and learned how to feed and bath Elias so that very soon it felt natural to be a mother. Takis visited every day. He brought her flowers and gave her a beautiful sapphire-and-diamond bracelet, but what she really wanted was for him to kiss her instead of prowling around her hospital room like a caged tiger. His edginess made her edgy, which in turn made the baby cry, and she was relieved when he left.

'Do you want to hold him?' she asked when they had brought Elias home, a month after his birth. Takis had carried the baby in his car seat up to the nursery. He shook his head when Lissa carefully lifted the baby out of the seat.

'Let him settle into his new environment. I expect you will need to feed and change him.' Takis was already at the door. 'I'll tell the nanny to come and help.'

Lissa frowned. Takis had only held Elias a couple of times, and on both occasions he had seemed reluctant to do so and had handed him back to her after a couple of minutes. But the baby was so tiny and fragile, and she supposed that Takis felt nervous. Initially she had argued against having a nanny, but Maria was an invaluable help, especially as Elias needed feeding during the night.

Lissa was sleeping in the bedroom adjoining the nursery, and at first she was so wrapped up in motherhood that she did not allow herself to wonder why Takis showed little interest in his son. He had gone back to his old habit of disappearing into his study when he was at home, and he went to his office every day, often working until late.

But as another month passed, his indifference became more apparent. Lissa blamed herself because the good relationship they'd established before Elias was born had cooled to the point where she and Takis rarely saw each other. If only she had not confessed her feelings for him, they might have been able to resume their marriage, which hadn't been perfect but had been better than the divisions between them, which she had no idea how to deal with. They were still sleeping separately, even though Elias had settled to one nightly feed, which the nanny gave him.

Lissa did not have the confidence to move back into the bedroom she had once shared with Takis, and he did not suggest it.

Her insecurities flooded back. Why had she forgotten that he had married her because she had been expecting his baby? A baby he took as little interest in as he did her, Lissa thought bleakly. She remembered how Takis had insisted that she was his responsibility. He had married her out of duty, and all the time in Santorini, when she had been falling in love with him, she had meant nothing to him.

Worst of all, he had broken his promise to love his baby. Although, when she thought back, she realised that Takis had never actually made that promise. He had said he would give his son his name and the benefits of his wealth. That he would protect him. But that wasn't the same and it wasn't enough, Lissa thought, anger replacing her deep hurt.

She imagined a future where she was desperate for Takis to take notice of her. Desperate for his affection and love until bitterness crept into her heart and she despised him as surely as he would despise her. Something broke inside her then. It wasn't selfish to want to be loved. With hindsight she realised that when she'd been a teenager and still grieving for her parents, she had needed her grandfather to love her. She deserved so much more. And now she knew what she must do. She must save herself from her loveless marriage that broke her heart daily.

* * *

Takis let himself into the house and dropped the bunch of flowers that he'd bought on his way home from the office on the hall table. The flowers were a peace offering that he hoped would break the impasse between him and Lissa. She had looked so unhappy lately and he knew he was responsible.

She did not understand why he had distanced himself from her and Elias, and he could not explain that he was protecting them. And, if he was honest, he was protecting himself. She had once taunted him that he was afraid of her, and it was true. He recognised that he was in danger of becoming attached to her.

The only way he could control emotions that he did not want was to put up barriers. He'd thought she hadn't noticed. But lately he had caught her looking at him with a vulnerable expression in her eyes that made his heart clench. She wanted more than he could give her, and they were going to have to negotiate a way around that for both their sakes.

He checked the ground-floor rooms before going upstairs to the nursery, expecting Lissa to be there. Elias was asleep in his crib. Takis glanced at the baby who reminded him so painfully of Giannis and quickly left the room. He found Lissa in the bedroom where she'd slept since she'd brought Elias home from the hospital. She stiffened when she glanced over her shoulder and saw him.

'I wasn't expecting you home so early,' she said flatly.

Takis roved his gaze over her slender figure. She looked amazing in jeans and a T-shirt, and it was hard to believe that she had given birth only two months ago. He wondered what she would do if he tumbled her down on the bed and removed their clothes before making fierce love to her. Sometimes he'd caught her giving him a hungry look that made him think she wanted to resume their physical relationship as much as he did.

It was then that he noticed the suitcase on the bed and the pile of clothes next to it. Foreboding dropped into the pit of his stomach. 'What is happening?'

'My sister has invited me to stay with her and Jace in Thessaloniki. I've only seen baby Acacia a couple of times and it will be nice for Elias to meet his cousin. Jace is sending his plane.'

Takis couldn't explain the relief that rushed through him. 'I should have thought to arrange the trip. You will enjoy spending time with Eleanor.'

Lissa closed the zip on the suitcase. 'Yes. And when I come back to Athens I want a divorce.'

He jerked his head back as if she'd slapped him. His heart was thudding painfully hard. 'I don't understand, *koúkla mou*,' he said carefully.

'*Don't* call me that,' she snapped, her eyes blazing. 'I'm not your doll. We both know that I am not anything to you.'

'That's not true.' He felt like he was standing in

a field of landmines and an explosion could wipe him out at any moment. 'You are my wife, and the mother of my son.'

'You wanted neither.' Her mouth trembled and she looked away from him and stuffed a sweatshirt into the suitcase. 'I could cope with your indifference if it only affected me, but it will affect our son. I won't let Elias grow up wondering why his papa doesn't love him. It's too cruel.' She dashed a hand across her eyes. 'I'm going to take him back to England. I'll find a job in hotel management that hopefully offers accommodation, and you won't have to see us ever again.'

Takis felt the walls of his fortress start to crumble. 'That is not what we agreed.'

'I know our marriage was meant to be a practical solution when I became pregnant,' she said in a strained voice. 'But it's not working for me and I have to end it.'

Fear cracked through him. 'Tell me what I have to do to make it work,' he gritted, unable to control his desperation that made him feel physically sick when he realised that she was serious about leaving him.

Tears shimmered in Lissa's eyes, but there was determination on her face, determination to leave him and take their child with her. 'You have to love me. And we both know that's not going to happen.'

Takis stared at her. 'We can work this out...'

'How?' she choked. 'I love you, and it's tearing me apart to know that you don't love me. I understand why after Giannis died you shut off your emotions. But another little boy needs your love. Elias is your son, but you ignore him, and it breaks my heart to think he would suffer the pain of rejection that I felt when my grandfather had no time for me.' Lissa lifted her chin. 'And I deserve more than a sham of a marriage.'

Takis silently applauded the self-confident woman she had become. The one who stood up for herself, for her son.

'I deserve to be loved,' she said fiercely. 'I want my freedom so that one day I can fall in love with someone who will love me back unreservedly.'

She walked over to the door. 'I forgot to bring Elias's car seat from downstairs. He will wake from his nap soon, and I have booked a taxi to take us to the airport.'

Takis watched her leave the room. He was frozen inside, and his lungs burned as he dragged in a breath. He ran a shaky hand over his eyes. Lissa had told him that she loved him, and in the next breath announced that she was leaving him. So was her first statement a lie? Just like his stepmother had lied about loving him all those years ago?

But the schoolboy infatuation he'd felt for Marina was nothing like the powerful feelings he had for Lissa. The truth hit him like a thunderbolt. Love. He had denied it and assured himself that he was in control of his emotions. Love hurt. Why would he risk the searing pain he'd felt when his brother had died? Instead he had been a coward and withheld his love from his baby son.

He strode down the corridor, opened the door to the nursery and walked across the room to the crib. A pair of blue eyes surveyed him unblinkingly, and then Elias smiled and Takis felt his heart shatter into a thousand pieces.

'I stayed away from you because I was scared,' he told the baby rawly. His throat felt like he'd swallowed broken glass. 'Scared I might drop you or do something wrong.' He swallowed hard. 'Scared to be your papa because I don't know how to be a father. But I will learn. I promised your mama that I will love and protect you always.'

Life was about choices, Lissa had said. Takis chose not to be a monster like his father had been. Chose to learn from his mistakes. He would be the best father he could be, he promised Elias. Taking a deep breath, he reached into the crib and carefully scooped his son into his arms.

The baby was so small and breakable. Was he holding him tightly enough? Too tight? Takis slowly released his breath and held Elias against his shoulder. The baby's dark hair felt like silk and he smelled…of baby, Takis thought as tenderness swept through him, and a wave of love so strong that it hurt his heart.

Lissa had said that he must forgive himself for Giannis's death in the fire that Takis now accepted had been an accident that he could not have prevented. He had punished himself for twenty years and buried his heart in an icy tomb. But the ice had gradually thawed in the warmth of Lissa's smiles and the light that blazed in her eyes when she looked at him. Only him.

'Your mama is wise and beautiful, and you have her eyes,' he told his son. He looked towards the door and saw the nanny holding a bottle of formula.

'Would you like to feed the baby?' she asked, offering Takis the bottle.

Not this time, but he had a lifetime to bond with his son, and he would, Takis vowed. 'I'll leave Elias with you,' he told the nanny. 'I have something important to tell my wife.'

Lissa walked back into the bedroom with the baby carrier and stopped dead when she saw Takis unpacking her suitcase. Her emotions couldn't take much more. She felt raw and did not even bother to wipe away the tears that coursed down her cheeks. She put the carrier on the floor and sagged against the door frame.

'Don't,' she choked. 'Just don't. I need to go.' She forced herself to look at him and her stupid heart broke all over again. He was so gorgeous, but he didn't want her, he'd never wanted her, except for on one perfect night. She sniffed inelegantly and knew she must look a mess. Her mascara wasn't waterproof, and she had cried enough tears to fill an ocean. 'You have taken everything else. Can't you at least let me have my dignity?'

'I love you.'

Her heart skittered as Takis said the words she'd longed to hear. But she shook her head. He was only saying them because she was leaving.

'No,' she said with tremulous effort. 'Don't play games with me.' Takis had said those words to her more than once. He had been suspicious of her and so furious about her pregnancy. More tears filled her eyes when she thought of darling little Elias, who would never have his father's love.

She pressed her finger against her quivering lips, hating that she was falling apart in front of Takis. She was aware of him moving and tensed when he drew her hand away from her mouth. He was so close that she breathed in his heavenly male scent, and she ached with longing.

'I knew I was in trouble the minute I saw you,' he said heavily. 'I'm not a big fan of weddings, but I couldn't refuse when Jace asked me to be his best man. All eyes were on the bride, except for mine. You stole my breath.'

He let go of her fingers, which he had been squeezing hard like a drowning man clinging to a life raft, and lifted his hand to brush her long fringe off her face. 'You stole my heart. I fell in love with you, but I fought my feelings and insisted that our marriage was a solution to a problem.'

'My pregnancy was a problem for you,' she said dully.

The expression in Takis's eyes made her tremble. 'I told myself that I did not deserve to be happy, but even that was an excuse. The truth is that I was afraid to acknowledge how I felt about you because all I knew of love was that it had nearly broken me. When Giannis died I made a pact with myself never to allow love into my life. I didn't need it, and I certainly didn't want it. But I couldn't forget you.'

He ran his finger lightly down her cheek, tracing the path of a tear. 'I thought if I kept you at arm's length I would be able to control what is in here.' He pressed his hand against his chest. 'But my heart knew the truth, *agapi mou*, and it beats only for you.'

'Takis.' She could not speak when her heart was beating so hard it hurt.

'If I beg, will you give me a chance to try to win back your love?'

She swallowed. 'I can't.'

Takis paled beneath his tan and closed his eyes. 'I'm sorry for how I treated you. I know I don't deserve your love.' He pinched the bridge of his nose and Lissa's heart turned over when she saw that his eyelashes were wet.

'It wouldn't be fair to Elias. I can't bear the thought of him feeling worthless because his father doesn't love him.'

'I adore our son,' he said urgently. 'I swear I will

spend the rest of my life making sure that he knows how special he is.'

Takis slipped his hand under her chin and gently tilted her face up to his. 'You humble me with your courage. You were heartbroken when your parents died, but you are willing to love again. I have seen your devotion to Elias, and I wish…' He swallowed hard.

He tried to smile and failed. 'Big boys do cry. Especially when they have lost the person they love most in all the world, the universe.'

Finally, Lissa believed him. 'You haven't lost me, my love,' she said softly. 'I am right here, and that's where I want to stay, forever.'

He kissed her then, with such tenderness, such *love* that Lissa felt as though her heart would burst.

'I love you,' she whispered against his mouth as he drew her down on to the bed.

'You are my world. You and Elias.' The reverence in Takis's eyes filled Lissa with joy. 'You are everything and I am nothing without you,' he said deeply.

They undressed each other with hands that trembled, and Takis told her over and over again how much he loved her before he worshipped her body with his mouth until she could wait no longer and lifted her hips towards him. When he entered her and made them one, it was like the first time, beautiful and new and shining, and Lissa was dazzled by this love of theirs that was brighter than the brightest star and would blaze until the end of time.

* * *

A week later, the helicopter flew over Santorini, but instead of going to the villa it landed in the grounds of the Aphrodite hotel. The hotel had not opened for guests yet, so Lissa was surprised to see several cars parked on the driveway.

'Maria will take Elias for a walk in the pram,' Takis told her as he ushered her into the hotel.

'Is an event taking place here today?' Lissa asked.

'A wedding.' His eyes gleamed with an expression she could not decipher. It did not happen often for they no longer had secrets from each other.

She walked into the wedding room and saw that a long table was set with delicate crockery, champagne flutes and a stunning floral display down the centre of the damask tablecloth. The pure white roses intertwined with spikes of purple lavender and sprigs of fragrant rosemary were exactly what she would have chosen for her dream wedding, Lissa thought wistfully.

Outside on the terrace, chairs had been arranged in rows facing the arbour, which was swathed in white voile and decorated with roses. Beyond the romantic arch was that amazing view of the caldera, and the sky and the sea were as blue as the sapphire on Lissa's engagement ring.

It was astonishing how the bride, whoever she was, had incorporated every detail that Lissa had drawn on her designs when she'd planned the wedding venue.

'I hope I haven't forgotten anything,' Takis murmured. 'I used your designs to create the wedding setting.'

'I hope the bride approves,' she said lightly, trying not to show her disappointment that another woman would enjoy *her* perfect wedding.

Takis smiled. 'I hope she does too.' He captured her hands and linked his fingers through hers. She was stunned when he dropped down on to one knee. 'Will you marry me, Lissa *mou*? Here, today, in front of our family and friends, and will you let me show you how deeply I love you for the rest of our lives? All of this...' he glanced around at the beautiful wedding setting '...is for you, for us, so that you can have the wedding of your dreams.'

'B-but we are already married,' she stammered.

'The ceremony will be a blessing of our marriage and a renewal of the vows we made to one another.'

'Oh, Takis, I love you so much.'

'I love you, *kardia mou*.' He framed her face with his hands and lowered his mouth to hers to kiss her with tender devotion.

'Are we really going to have a wedding ceremony today?' Lissa asked several blissful minutes later when he trailed his lips over her cheek and nuzzled the tender spot behind her ear.

'We are.'

She gave a rueful glance down at her strap top and denim skirt. 'I'm not dressed to be a bride.'

'I left your sister to organise your wedding dress

and she delivered it to the hotel just before you arrived. Your brother is here too.'

'Eleanor is here in Santorini? Did she know you were planning all this?'

'I needed her help so that I could make our wedding perfect.'

She smiled at him through her tears. 'I thought you were not a fan of weddings?'

'I will love ours, because I love you, *koúkla mou*, and I'll do anything to make you happy.'

'That's easy. You just have to keep loving me.'

Takis caught hold of her hand and led her up to the honeymoon suite. 'Your dress is hanging in the wardrobe. I am under strict orders from your sister not to take a look at it.'

'How long do we have before the ceremony?' Lissa murmured. She met his smouldering gaze and recognised his hunger, which was as urgent as hers.

'Just long enough,' he growled as he scooped her up into his arms and carried her over to the bed. And then he was kissing her like she had longed to be kissed, wildly and passionately, his tongue tangling with hers while his hands made short work of undressing her.

She felt the thunder of his heart beneath her fingertips when she skimmed her hands over his chest, tracing the arrowing of rough hairs down to where his arousal was thick and hard. When he eased into her, he told her how much he loved her. He kept nothing back as he whispered the secrets that were no longer hidden in his heart and were all for her.

Later that afternoon, Lissa stared at her reflection in the mirror and decided that this must be a dream. Her wedding dress was from the pages of a fairy tale, an exquisite concoction of ivory tulle and lace with an off-the-shoulder bodice and a full skirt adorned with tiny pearls and diamanté. Her brother, Mark, escorted her down to the terrace where her friends from England had gathered with Takis's friends, who had welcomed her into their social circle in Athens. Eleanor was there with Jace and their baby daughter, and Elias was asleep in his pram.

Her eyes flew to Takis, who looked impossibly handsome in a light grey suit, a navy blue shirt and silvery grey tie. Her husband who loved her. It was in his eyes when he gazed at her in a kind of awe, and in his husky voice when he whispered that she was the most beautiful bride there had ever been.

When they renewed their vows he slid a stunning diamond eternity ring on to her finger, where it sparkled as brightly as stars next to the blue sapphire engagement ring and her wedding band.

'The honeymoon suite has a pool where we can swim beneath the stars,' Takis whispered against her lips.

'I didn't pack my swimsuit.'

He grinned. 'Neither did I.'

* * *

Dinner was a noisy, happy affair as the wedding party laughed and chatted and toasted the health and happiness of the bride and groom. It was all a little too much for the youngest guests, and as the sun sank into the sea and the sky turned pink and gold, Takis carried his son across the terrace to show him the breathtaking sunset.

Jace was there, cradling his little daughter in his arms. 'Do you remember how we used to say that we would never get married, and we definitely didn't want children? What happened?' he asked ruefully.

'Love happened.' Takis grinned. 'We have come a long way, my friend. Who would have guessed that we would end up with our own families?'

'I have no regrets,' Jace said. 'How about you?'

'I am the luckiest man in the world.' Takis looked down at his angelic son before he turned his head and gazed at his wife, who was the love of his life. She looked over at him and her smile was full of love and promise for tonight when they would be alone. 'No regrets,' he said softly.

* * * * *

COMING NEXT MONTH FROM

PRESENTS

#3945 HER BEST KEPT ROYAL SECRET
Heirs for Royal Brothers
by Lynne Graham

Independent Gaby thought nothing could be more life-changing than waking up in the bed of the playboy prince who was so dangerous to her heart... Until she's standing in front of Angel a year later, sharing her shocking secret—his son!

#3946 CROWNED FOR HIS DESERT TWINS
by Clare Connelly

To become king, Sheikh Khalil must marry...immediately. But first, a mind-blowing whirlwind night with India McCarthy that neither can resist! When India reveals she's pregnant, can a ring secure his crown...and his heirs?

#3947 FORBIDDEN TO HER SPANISH BOSS
The Acostas!
by Susan Stephens

Rose Kelly can't afford any distractions. Especially her devilishly attractive boss, Raffa Acosta! But a week of networking on his superyacht may take them from professional to dangerously passionate territory...

#3948 SHY INNOCENT IN THE SPOTLIGHT
The Scandalous Campbell Sisters
by Melanie Milburne

Elspeth's sheltered existence means she's hesitant to swap places with her exuberant twin for a glamorous wedding. But the social spotlight is nothing compared to the laser focus of cynical billionaire Mack's undivided attention...

#3949 PROOF OF THEIR ONE HOT NIGHT
The Infamous Cabrera Brothers
by Emmy Grayson
One soul-stirring night with notorious tycoon Alejandro leaves Calandra pregnant. She plans to raise the baby alone. He's determined to prove he's parent material—and tempt her into another smoldering encounter...

#3950 HOW TO TEMPT THE OFF-LIMITS BILLIONAIRE
South Africa's Scandalous Billionaires
by Joss Wood
On a mission to acquire Roisin's South African vineyard, tycoon Muzi knows he needs to keep his eyes on the business deal, not his best friend's sister. Only, their forbidden temptation leads to even more forbidden nights...

#3951 THE ITALIAN'S BRIDE ON PAPER
by Kim Lawrence
When arrogant billionaire Samuele arrives at her door announcing his claim to her nephew, he sends Maya's senses into overdrive... She refuses to leave the baby's side, so he demands more—her as his convenient wife!

#3952 REDEEMED BY HIS NEW YORK CINDERELLA
by Jadesola James
Kitty will do anything for the foundation inspired by her tumultuous childhood. Even agree to a fake relationship to help Laurence, the impossibly guarded man from her past, land his next deal. Only, their chemistry is anything but make-believe!

YOU CAN FIND MORE INFORMATION ON UPCOMING HARLEQUIN TITLES, FREE EXCERPTS AND MORE AT HARLEQUIN.COM.

HPCNMRB0921

Kitty will do anything for the foundation inspired by her tumultuous childhood. Even agree to a fake relationship to help Laurence, the impossibly guarded man from her past, land his next deal. Only, their chemistry is anything but make-believe!

Read on for a sneak preview of debut author Jadesola James's new story for Harlequin Presents, Redeemed by His New York Cinderella.

"I'll speak plainly." The way he should have in the beginning, before she had him ruminating.

"All right."

"I'm close to signing the man you met. Giles Mueller. He's the owner of the Mueller Racetrack."

She nodded.

"You know it?"

"It's out on Long Island. I attended an event close to it once."

He grunted. "The woman you filled in for on Friday is—was—my set date for several events over the next month. Since Giles already thinks you're her, I'd like you to step in. In exchange, I'll make a handsome donation to your charity—"

"Foundation."

"Whatever you like."

There was silence between them for a moment, and Katherine looked at him again. It made him uncomfortable at once. He knew she couldn't see into his mind, but there was something very perceptive about that look. She said nothing, and he continued talking to cover the silence.

"You see, Katherine, I owe you a debt." Laurence's voice was dry. "You saved my life, and in turn I'll save your business."

She snorted. "What makes you think my business needs saving?"

Laurence laughed incredulously. "You're a one-person operation. You don't even have an office. Your website is one of those ghastly pay-by-the-month templates. You live in a boardinghouse—"

"I don't need an office," Katherine said proudly. "I meet clients in restaurants and coffee shops. An office is an old-fashioned and frankly completely unneeded expense. I'm not looking to make money off this, Laurence. I want to help people. Not everyone is like you."

Laurence chose not to pursue the insult; what mattered was getting Katherine to sign. "As you like," he said dismissively, then reached for his phone. "My driver has the paperwork waiting in the car. I'll have him bring it around now—"

"No."

It took a moment for the word to register. "Excuse me?"

Katherine did not repeat herself, but she did shake her head. "It's a kind offer, Laurence," she said firmly, "but the thought of playing your girlfriend is at least as absurd as your lie was."

Laurence realized after several seconds had passed that he was gaping, and he closed his mouth rapidly. He'd anticipated many different counteroffers—all that had been provided for in the partnership proposal that was ready for her to sign—but a refusal was something he was wholly unprepared for.

"You're saying no?" he said, to clarify.

She nodded.

"Why the hell would you say no?" The question came out far more harshly than he would have liked, but he was genuinely shocked. "You have everything to gain."

Don't miss
Redeemed by His New York Cinderella,
available October 2021 wherever
Harlequin Presents books and ebooks are sold.

Harlequin.com